Authors:

LEO BANKS

STAN SMITH

LARRY STARKEY

JOE STOCKER

KATHERINE GEHM

Book Editor: BOB ALBANO

# DAYS *of* DESTINY

C O N T E N T S

Design: MARY WINKELMAN VELGOS    Copy Editors: EVELYN HOWELL
Illustrations: GARY BENNETT                       CHARLES BURKHART
Back cover art: KEVIN KIBSEY

---

Prepared by the Book Division of *Arizona Highways*® magazine, a monthly publication of the Arizona Department of Transportation.

Publisher — Nina M. La France
Managing Editor — Bob Albano
Associate Editor — Robert J. Farrell
Art Director — Mary Winkelman Velgos
Production Director — Cindy Mackey

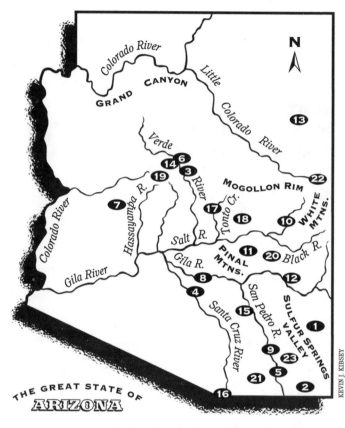

THE GREAT STATE OF
ARIZONA

KEVIN J. KIBSEY

## L E G E N D

| | | |
|---|---|---|
| 1. Apache Pass | 9. Fairbank | 17. Payson |
| 2. Bisbee | 10. Fort Apache | 18. Pleasant Valley |
| 3. Camp Verde | 11. Globe | 19. Prescott/Ft. Wipple |
| 4. Casa Grande | 12. Geronimo | 20. San Carlos |
| 5. Charleston | 13. Holbrook | 21. Sonoita Valley |
| 6. Clarkdale | 14. Jerome | 22. Springerville |
| 7. Congress | 15. Mammoth | 23. Tombstone |
| 8. Florence | 16. Nogales | |

**D**ays of Destiny is a collection of stories by contributors to *Arizona Highways* about lawmen and desperados and their feats and atrocities.

Some of these days loom as pivotal — a cheating card dealer is fired and four people die; Apaches capture a boy and he emerges years later as a feared, vicious Army scout; a woman down on her luck robs a stagecoach, but ends up on a pedestal; a body is found and the West's last great manhunt begins.

Other days mark the end, brought by a bullet or rope.

Sixteen of the stories were researched and written by Tucsonan Leo Banks, a journalist who specializes in Western history. He wrote these chapters: *Johnny Behind-the-Deuce, Morgan Earp, Warren Earp, Bob Paul, Last Manhunt, Jim Roberts, Woman Killer, Mickey Free, Tombstone's Last Hanging, Mass Lynching, Catalina Kid, Bronco Billy, Three-Fingered Jack Dunlap, Black Jack Ketchum, Bill Smith,* and *The Globe Fiends.*

*Buckskin Frank Leslie* is by Larry Starkey. *Pearl Hart* is by Stan Smith. *Burt Mossman* was adapted from a story by Phoenix writer Joe Stocker that was published in the magazine. The chapter *Billy Claibourne* (his last name is spelled various ways in reference materials) was adapted from a story by Katherine Gehm.

# CHAPTER ONE

# BUCKSKIN FRANK LESLIE

They wrote no songs or books
about "Buckskin" Frank Leslie's exploits.
But he probably was the deadliest of gunfighters
attracted to Tombstone
in the years following the first big strike
on that "hill of silver" rising above
the San Pedro River.
His four, and possibly five, known killings
were considered an incomplete count
by his contemporaries, who marveled
at his skill with a six-gun. They believed
he was responsible for the deaths of as many as a
dozen more men left lying in the desert, including
that of the infamous Johnny Ringo.
For most of the 1880s,
he was a feared gunfighter. But on

*July 4, 1889,*

Leslie got drunk and stayed drunk for a week.
When he sobered up, he was in jail, and headed
for a term in the Yuma Territorial Prison.

Calling himself Nashville F. Leslie, he arrived in Tombstone in the early summer of 1880 wearing deerskin breeches and jacket made famous only four years earlier as General Custer's garb at the Little Big Horn. The first documented evidence of his presence is a notice in the *Nugget* on June 10, saying he had taken employment as a bartender in the Cosmopolitan Hotel, where he also had a room.

Although the former Army scout had exchanged his frontier attire for the clothing of a gentleman, he continued to wear a vest tailored of deerskin, taking pride in the nickname by which he would be remembered.

In less than two weeks, "Buckskin Frank" Leslie was noticed again by the newspapers, this time for making his first contribution to the town's famous Boothill cemetery. The *Tombstone Epitaph* of June 22 reported a gunfight at the Cosmopolitan during which two slugs hit Mike Killeen — another bartender at the hotel.

Frank Leslie readily accepted responsibility for the shooting.

On the night of the shooting, Leslie was seated alongside Mrs. May Killeen on the porch of the Cosmopolitan when her estranged husband appeared. He had previously warned them to stay apart, and this time fists as well as words were exchanged.

Mike Killeen fired at least one shot that glanced off Leslie's skull (Frank would claim two). Then the rivals grappled again, Killeen pistol-whipping his fellow bartender before delivering similar punishment to a friend of Leslie's named George Perrine. During the scuffling, which led from the porch to a hallway of the hotel, Killeen was shot in the face, and then in the body.

Mike claimed both men had fired at him, but Leslie

told the jury Killeen had called him an S.O.B. "Naturally," he testified, "I had to protect myself, so I drew my gun and shot him in self-defense." The jury agreed, and on July 6 Frank Leslie and the not-so-grieving widow were married.

It's hard to find accounts of Tombstone life in those days without a reference to Leslie's skill with a gun. Many people believed Doc Holliday had turned away from taking him on. Others noted how Leslie often demonstrated his prowess with a pistol by shooting flies from the ceilings of saloons.

Tombstone was a hard-drinking town, and along with respect for Leslie's accuracy came a caution to give him a wide berth when he was in his cups.

Long before the fateful July 4, Mrs. May Leslie discovered how unpleasant Buckskin Frank could be when he mixed whiskey with gunpowder. Neighbors of the Leslies told of repeated nights of hysteria after Frank's drinking sessions. He would stand her against a wall, raise his revolver, and outline her terrified body with bullet holes to prove that his aim, if not his judgment, was unaffected by booze.

It was the kind of story guaranteed to bring him respect from his peers.

For a few months after the Killeen shooting, Leslie's life seemed to be settling into a relatively peaceful pattern. On September 20, 1880, he was reported prospecting in Cochise Pass, and he would file several valuable claims. By November 29, he had taken employment as a bartender in the Oriental Saloon, owned by Milt Joyce and Wyatt Earp, and was granted the power of arrest on its premises by the City Council. He was becoming a solid citizen.

Even the Earp-supporting *Epitaph* editorially congratulated Leslie and the young widow on their marriage.

By January 14, 1881, the Leslies were doing well enough for him to order a custom Colt .44 revolver with a 12-inch barrel, "superior finished throughout with carved ivory handles."

Success in respectable circles, however, wasn't enough for Buckskin Frank.

In March 1881, he became an opportunist working both sides of the rivalry between the "reformers" who supported the Earps, and the "cowboy faction" backing Sheriff John Behan. A "reform" posse selected him as its guide after an attempted stage robbery had resulted in the senseless murders of two men. That was seven months before the feud between the two factions led to the gunfight at the O.K. Corral on October 26, 1881.

One member of the posse remembered Leslie as a fine singer, a good storyteller, and a welcome companion. Another grumbled that for a fellow who had claimed to be General Crook's chief of scouts he was a lousy tracker.

He had misled the posse to protect friends in the "cowboy faction," and admitted it to Earp years later.

Whether it can be proved that Leslie actually rode with the Johnny Ringo-Curly Bill gang, contemporary accounts agree he spent increasing amounts of time in their company. This was bad for them, since he also was an informant for Wells Fargo.

In later years, Wyatt Earp said Buckskin Frank was paid to keep close watch on Ringo. The Wells Fargo undercover agent in Tombstone, Fred Dodge, said it went beyond that. He said his company offered a bounty for the outlaw, alive or dead.

In the early afternoon of July 13, 1882 — the last day of Johnny Ringo's life — a shot was heard in the desert along the Barefoot Trail leading to Galeyville. Just before that, William Sanders, Sr., whose ranch was nearby, had seen Ringo ride past.

The outlaw had been drinking heavily for several days with two pals, Billy Claibourne and Frank Leslie. That is perhaps why Sanders thought little of it when he saw Leslie, some minutes behind but riding hard, spur his horse along the same trail. Another witness recalled Leslie pulling his heavily lathered mount into the O.K. Corral late that afternoon.

Fourteen men had seen Ringo's body, seated in the fork of a scrub oak on the bank of Turkey Creek, his .45 in his right hand and the death-wound in his right temple. One shot had been discharged from his revolver. The men did not specify whether black powder burns were visible around the wound, as would be likely in a suicide.

On November 13, 1882, four months after Ringo was killed, those 14 men signed a "Statement of Citizens in regard to the Death of John Ringo," which led the coroner to rule it was suicide. And, first thing the next morning, Ringo's pal Billy Claiborne got so mad that he made the mistake of calling Frank Leslie out into the street.

By 7 a.m. Claibourne was heading for the Oriental looking for trouble — and for Buckskin Frank. Although he hadn't hesitated to flee when the shooting started at the O.K. Corral, Claibourne now used "exceedingly offensive language" to confront a gunman he knew to be every bit as dangerous as Holliday or the Earps.

Thrown out of the saloon, Claibourne warned Leslie, "I'll get even with you." A few minutes later, informed that

Claibourne was approaching the Allen Street front door with his Winchester, Buckskin Frank calmly took a pistol from behind the bar and went out the Fifth Street side door, where he was seen to pause for a moment before moving cautiously to the corner.

"Billy, don't shoot," Leslie remembered saying, and, although he had taken his opponent by surprise, eyewitnesses agreed he gave Claibourne the first shot, which went wild. Leslie's shots never went wild.

"He raised his gun and shot, and I returned the shot from my pistol," Buckskin Frank would testify. "... I saw him double up and had my pistol cocked and aimed at him again."

But no second shot was required. Before he died, Billy Claibourne swore that Buckskin Frank Leslie had admitted being John Ringo's murderer. Years later, a Yuma Prison guard named Frank King also would claim that Buckskin Frank privately had confessed to the murder.

After the Claibourne shooting, Buckskin Frank was seen less often around Tombstone, although he still frequented the gin mills and the easy girls at 6th and Allen streets.

Tombstone was changing. Members of the "cowboy faction" either were dead or hiding from the Earps after back shooters had crippled Virgil and murdered Morgan after the O.K. Corral fight. The brothers, and Holliday, had fled Tombstone rather than face a jury inquiry concerning some of the killings that followed the attacks on Virgil and Morgan. John Slaughter would soon replace Behan as sheriff of the newly-created Cochise County. The silver mines, where production had peaked in 1882, would be flooding heavily two years later. Tombstone's half-decade of violence was over. Only Buckskin Frank Leslie remained from the old days. He signed on for a while as a dispatch rider for the Army, quit, then added a second hitch as a scout in May, 1885. For a while, he worked as a mounted customs inspector along the border.

Off and on, he had been running the Magnolia Ranch, about 25 miles east and a little south of Tombstone in the Swisshelm Mountains. The little cattle spread was owned by Milt Joyce, the majority owner of the Oriental, and when Joyce left for California, Frank Leslie took it over.

His personal life, too, was changing. On September 3, 1887, May Killeen Leslie won a divorce from him. Her legal papers cited not his pistol proclivities, but his numerous infidelities. Frank Leslie didn't contest the divorce. Not only had his drinking increased dramatically, but he had found a ready companion — blonde and buxom — for his bouts with booze. Her name was Mollie.

Mollie Williams/Edwards/Bradshaw (her last name apparently depended more on circumstance than ceremony) was a favorite of the crowd at the Bird Cage Theatre, to which she had been brought by E.L. Bradshaw. "Blonde Mollie's" singing voice as much as her ample figure had drawn the attention of many — although not quite all, since the story is told that Buckskin Frank, irritated by an inattentive cowboy dangling his leg over one of the Bird Cage's infamous "private" balconies, had shot off the offender's boot heel.

"Brad" Bradshaw is remembered for two reasons. He shot and killed T.J. Waters in a dispute over the color of a shirt, and his body was found one morning in a Tombstone alley shortly after Frank Leslie became interested in "Blonde Mollie."

This had apparently become Frank's idea of a proposal, and Mollie promptly moved in with him at the Magnolia Ranch. They became compatible, in their way, continually drinking and brawling and no doubt making up and loving — until Independence Day, 1889.

That's when Buckskin Frank Leslie, joined by Mollie, started a drinking episode that began in Tombstone and lasted a week, until the night he dropped her off at the ranch and decided to "clean out the whole valley."

After failing to goad a neighbor into a gunfight, even throwing down a spare revolver and unsuccessfully challenging the man to pick it up, he rode home firing at the clouds and the stars and the moon and the sagebrush, arriving at his little ranch house in Horseshoe Valley still looking for something to kill.

Whether "Blonde Mollie" and their part-time ranch hand, a young man who liked to be called "Six-gun Jimmy" Neil, did anything to provoke him will never be known. Leslie would claim Mollie had a gun, although there's no reason to believe him, and if she did it was of little use. Like May Killeen Leslie years before, Mollie was nothing more than a target, although this time his aim would prove to be more deadly. "I'll settle this," Neil remembered him yelling, just before the gun came into play.

Mollie died instantly from the first shot, which passed through her chest from left to right. Two more bullets were promptly pumped into Six-gun Jimmy, who may have had a gun or may have had a romantic interest in Mollie, but who had no chance to defend himself or Mollie.

Then, the violence and his adrenaline spent, Leslie

passed out in a drunken stupor.

Although hit in the arm and body, Neil would live a couple more years. While Leslie slept off his drunk, Six-gun Jimmy crawled a mile and a half to the house of a neighbor, who fetched Tombstone's Dr. Goodfellow and then went for the law.

The next morning, his judgment blurred by a hangover, Buckskin Frank mounted up and headed for Tombstone. On the way, he met the lawmen sent to bring him in. He told them Jimmy had killed Mollie before Leslie, in self-defense, could put him down. It wasn't much of a story. But the posse pretended to believe him, and Leslie peacefully handed over his guns.

The gunfighter stubbornly stuck to his story for a while, but he was faced with a noose if Jimmy Neil took the stand against him. So he copped a plea, and in January 1890 joined 10 other prisoners being escorted west by Sheriff Slaughter to the Yuma Territorial Prison, perched on a high bluff overlooking the Colorado River.

Near the prison, the Southern Pacific Hotel offered a bar for weary travelers, and the sheriff saw nothing untoward about pausing there for a while with his prisoners. After washing away enough trail dust, newspapers reported, Buckskin Frank Leslie needed assistance to stagger through the prison's entrance to begin a term that would last nearly seven years.

Punished with time in the "dark cell" for an aborted prison break two months after his arrival in Yuma, Frank Leslie became a model prisoner, serving as the institution's pharmacist and even being commended for risking his own health to care for the sick during numerous epidemics.

On December 2, 1893, the *San Francisco Chronicle*

published a lengthy interview with Leslie accompanied by a photograph, and a local divorcee named Belle Stowell initiated correspondence. Nearly three years later, following the submission of clemency requests by numerous prominent citizens, Governor Benjamin J. Franklin granted him a full pardon on November 17, 1896. Two weeks later, Frank and Belle were married, telling the newspapers they planned a honeymoon in China.

There is no further word of either of them, although a Frank Leslie is listed as manager of a San Francisco grocery store in 1904-5, and a California newspaper claimed to have interviewed the old gunfighter about 1920. In the article, Leslie supposedly confessed to the Ringo killing. It also speculated that Leslie committed suicide in the hills north of Martinez, California.

There are legends of Leslie leading parties into Mexico and finding riches in the Yukon. As late as 1948, an old man named Barney McCoy, just before he died in a San Diego hospital, claimed to be Buckskin Frank Leslie.

A letter purportedly penned by the gunfighter himself at the age of 106 was postmarked Logan County, Kentucky, bordering the Tennessee city of Nashville from which Leslie chose his formal name. The three-page handwritten letter, in its closing paragraphs, provides the most fitting epitaph not only for Buckskin Frank Leslie but for Tombstone itself, and for the few years when the last of the Western gunfighters gathered there:

"Some people may say Wayte (sic) Earp cleaned up Tombstone. Some may say John Behan. I don't think either did. It just dried up."

# JOHNNY BEHIND-THE-DEUCE

Fate sometimes seems to make odd choices
when it parcels out immortality.
One of them was Michael O'Rourke,
a drifter and gambler often described
as a runt and a tinhorn. But he was
not to pass from the scene without leaving
an indelible ripple on Tombstone.
At about noon on a snapping cold

## January 14, 1881,

O'Rourke fatally shot a
prominent mining engineer in the head,
touching off a sequence of events that keep
historians arguing to this day.

Michael O'Rourke drifted into Tombstone about 1879. They called him "Johnny Behind-the-Deuce" because when playing faro he bet heavily if his hole card was a deuce. The nickname carried the whiff of legend.

The pace of the legend quickened in the aftermath of the shooting and the reported involvement of Wyatt Earp in saving O'Rourke from a lynch mob. In the hands of Earp biographer, Stuart Lake, Wyatt's role became Herculean. Lake, a master storyteller, stacked this one high, writing:

"Wyatt threw his shotgun before him, left hand on the fore-end, right on grip and triggers. In the crowd every man had a shotgun, rifle, or six-gun, ready to pour lead into the lone peace officer ... 'Stop where you are,' Wyatt ordered. ... 'One step more and you get it' "

At Wyatt's death in 1929, the headline of his obituary in the *Tombstone Epitaph* said he was most remembered for two events — the fight at the O.K. Corral and his rescue of Johnny Behind-the-Deuce.

However, many writers have claimed there was no credible threat of a lynching. Others believe the real hero was Tombstone Marshal Ben Sippy.

The facts of events that day might be clouded, but it is possible, through the words of eyewitnesses and contemporary newspapers, to piece together a likely account.

The murder occurred in Charleston, a mill town on the San Pedro River where ore from Tombstone was pounded into bullion. Henry Schneider, chief engineer of the Tombstone Mining and Milling Company, was on a lunch break when he entered Smith's restaurant and went to the fireplace. According to an account in the *Epitaph* for January 15, 1881, Schneider spoke to a friend about the

temperature. O'Rourke, seated nearby, said, "I thought you never get cold."

"I was not talking to you, sir," Schneider snapped.

The *Epitaph* wrote: "This raised the lurking devil in the diminutive heart of 'Johnny Behind-the-Deuce,' who blurted out, 'God damn you, I'll shoot you when you come out,' and left the room.

"After eating his dinner, Mr. Schneider passed out the door, and was proceeding to the mill when, true to his promise, the lurking fiend, who had secreted himself with hell in his heart and death in his mind, drew deadly aim and dropped his victim in his tracks."

But the Deuce told a different story to the *Arizona Weekly Citizen*. He said that he and Schneider traded hot words, and the engineer lunged at him and called him an unprintable name. "There were some ladies in the restaurant, and it made me awful mad to be called that. I told him that I had too much respect for the ladies to fight in there, but to come out on the sidewalk."

Once outside, O'Rourke says, he was convinced to let the matter drop, and was heading for a saloon when Schneider charged outside, knife in hand.

"He continued to crowd against me and I pulled my gun and shot him," O'Rourke said. "I was so excited when I shot him that I dropped my revolver and ran."

Schneider's sudden end filled the streets with angry miners. Some historians contend that their mood was darkened more when some cowboys, eager for a hanging, plied the miners with booze in Cain's Saloon.

To protect his prisoner, Charleston's Constable George McKelvey hustled O'Rourke into a wagon and beat it for Tombstone, 10 miles away.

O'Rourke told the *Citizen* that after his arrest, "all the men rushed over from the mill and there was a terrible excitement. They said they would hold an inquest on Schneider, and if I killed him, they would hang me in 20 minutes."

This was confirmed in the diary of Tombstone resident George W. Parson, who wrote: "A gambler called Johnny Behind-the-Deuce ... rode into town followed by mounted men who chased him from Charleston, he having shot and killed Schneider."

In Lake's telling, Wyatt put the Deuce inside Vogan's bowling alley and saloon, with brothers Virgil and Morgan as guards. Then he cradled a sawed-off shotgun across his chest to face the outraged miners from Charleston and several hundred more from the company's mine on the hill above town.

According to Lake, Wyatt stood down 500 "bloodlusting frontiersmen" by glaring at Richard Gird, the mining company's owner and leader of the throng, and calmly saying, "Nice mob you've got, Gird. I didn't know you trailed with such company." After more such talk, Lake says, Gird was convinced of the foolishness of challenging Wyatt and turned away.

"While Wyatt Earp held the lynch mob at bay," Lake wrote, "Sheriff Johnny Behan, two of his deputies and Ben Sippy, the Tombstone marshal, stood across Allen Street from the bowling alley and made no move to assist Wyatt."

But the *Epitaph* story leads some to conclude that Earp's role was manufactured. The paper never mentioned Earp, and credited Ben Sippy with fast thinking in assembling a group of armed deputies and securing a wagon to transport the prisoner to Tucson. As the lawmen made their way down the street, they turned their rifles on the advancing mob, but resisted calls to open fire.

"But Marshal Sippy's sound judgment prevented any such outbreak as would have been the certain result," the *Epitaph* reported, "and cool as an iceberg he held the crowd in check. No one who was a witness to yesterday's proceedings can doubt that but for his presence, blood would have flown freely."

So which version holds the truth — Lake's with Wyatt as hero, or the *Epitaph's* claims for Sippy?

The temptation to endorse the *Epitaph* is strong, despite its feverish prose. After all, the story was written within hours of the event, not almost a half-century later.

But the Ben Sippy presented in the *Epitaph* is not the one known to Tombstone historians. As marshal, he was considered ineffective in controlling the rollicking silver camp. Sippy might have been a good man, but he was not one to take command in a crisis. Wyatt Earp was.

In his diary, Parsons wrote that lawmen on the scene

deputized numerous gambling men to help protect the Deuce. It's likely that Wyatt, who owned several faro tables at the Oriental Saloon, was among this group. Placing himself in a commanding position in the center of the storm on Allen Street would be characteristic of him.

His presence outside Vogan's that day, and his role in the Deuce's rescue, were mentioned by eyewitness Fred Dodge in his book, *Under Cover for Wells Fargo*.

Even Billy Breakenridge, whose 1927 book *Helldorado* trashed the Earps, gave a grudging salute to Wyatt for holding back the mob. "When the mob, increased by about an equal number of miners from the hill, came up to take Johnny Behind-the-Deuce away to hang him," Breakenridge wrote, "Earp stood them off with a shotgun, and dared them to come and get them."

But the best evidence of Wyatt's heroism that day might be the quality of Lake's research. While his stories might have been exaggerated to appeal to a 1931 audience eager for heroes, his basic research on the Tombstone story was good.

As for Wyatt himself, his best quote on the Deuce affair can be found in Walter Noble Burns' interview notes from his 1927 book, *Tombstone: An Iliad of the Southwest*: "I just held them off until they brought the wagon. That's all."

Deuce made it safely to the jail in Tucson. On the night of April 14, the killer escaped, and despite the dogged pursuit of Sheriff Charlie Shibell and three Indian trackers, was never heard from again.

But by then fate had made its choice, and Michael O'Rourke became immortal as Johnny Behind-the-Deuce.

# BILLY CLAIBOURNE

William Claibourne reveled in the nickname his cronies around Tombstone, Arizona, gave him. They called him "Billy the Kid" after New Mexico's William Bonney, alias Billy the Kid.

Billy seemed to feel obligated to live up to the name with displays of bravado. By then, he had survived an incident in which he flung himself onto a raging bull to save his boss's life. Later, he would kill a man, but be acquitted. He would duck into a building just before his buddies faced off against the Earps and Doc Holliday at the O.K. Corral. And he, Johnny Ringo and "Buckskin" Frank Leslie would engage in a days-long drinking spree after which Ringo was shot to death. But Billy did not evade fate on

*November 14, 1882,*

when he called out Buckskin Frank, the man he believed had killed Ringo.

Billy Claibourne was born in Louisiana in 1862. His father and Texas rancher John Slaughter were lifelong friends. When Billy was 17 he went to work for Slaughter to learn the cattle business.

Billy hadn't been at the job for long when Slaughter decided to move to Arizona Territory. So this young cowhand helped bring to San Pedro Valley the parent herd of one of the largest spreads to develop in southeastern Arizona — the famous San Bernardino Ranch that covered 65,000 acres and reached deep into Mexico.

As Claibourne was working cattle, Tombstone burst onto the scene, and, along with mining camps Charleston and Galeyville, provided cowboys with saloons and gambling halls. Although he got caught up in the bawdy pleasures associated with Tombstone, Billy Claibourne proved to be one of the most dependable ranch hands John Slaughter ever had. And, he saved his boss's life.

In the following years, John Slaughter, while he could not defend the young cowhand's rowdiness, would acknowledge: "I owe my life to Billy."

"It was during our drive to Arizona," Slaughter would explain. "A bull charged me and if Billy hadn't split the breeze and flung himself from the saddle onto the animal's horns, wrestled and thrown it, I sure wouldn't be here to tell the tale."

The story of Claibourne's courage spread. The young man would laugh off the talk of his bravery and say, "If I'd a-been killed it wouldn't have mattered, but John had a pretty young wife. And to make Mrs. Slaughter a widow after only a few weeks of marriage would have been just too bad."

In jest, Claibourne's friends bestowed the "Billy the

Kid" sobriquet on him. Eventually, Claibourne succumbed to his local fame and the bawdiness of the area. His pals included some of Tombstone's infamous characters — Johnny Ringo, Curly Bill Brocius, Ike and Billy Clanton, and Tom and Frank McLaury. Even before Tombstone sprung to life in 1879, these "cowboys" were robbing and rustling in southeastern Arizona, northern Mexico, and western New Mexico.

Claibourne's bravado seemed to intensify after July 1881, when Billy the Kid was shot to death in New Mexico. A few months later, on October 1, Claibourne, annoyed by a drunken heckler named James Hickey, gunned him down in front of a saloon. Because Hickey had been harassing Claibourne — Billy had even left one saloon for another to escape the heckling — Claibourne was acquitted at a trial in Tombstone.

Later that month, on October 26, 1881, Claibourne ducked into a building just before gunfire made the O.K. Corral an icon of the Wild West.

S everal months after the gunfight, Johnny Ringo's body was found not far from Tombstone. Ringo's body was seated in the fork of a scrub oak on the bank of Turkey Creek, his .45 in his right hand and the death-wound in his right temple. One shot had been discharged from his revolver.

On November 13, 1882, four months after Ringo was killed, 14 men signed a "Statement of Citizens in regard to the Death of John Ringo." The coroner then ruled Ringo had killed himself.

Billy believed Buckskin Frank killed Ringo. On the morning after the coroner's ruling he was drunk, and he was gunning for Frank Leslie, who was tending bar at the Oriental.

Claibourne staggered into the saloon, pushed himself into a group of men, and started insulting them. Leslie took Billy by the arm and pulled him to one side saying to "shut up or get out." As Claibourne started toward the door he yelled, "I'll see you later, Leslie".

Buckskin Frank answered, "As long as I'm around you can see me anytime."

And later, Billy stood outside the Oriental, drunk and noisy, informing the gathering crowd that his mission in Tombstone was to kill Buckskin Frank Leslie.

After several bystanders had gone into the Oriental to warn Leslie of Claibourne's threats, Leslie came out the side door of the saloon with a six-shooter. Billy fired twice and Buckskin Frank once.

Claibourne's shots missed. Leslie's hit Billy in the chest. Buckskin Frank prepared to fired again, but Billy called, "Don't shoot anymore, I'm killed." He died a few hours later. He was 20 years old, a year younger than Bonney, when he was shot down.

Leslie was acquitted. Billy the Kid Claibourne was buried in Tombstone's Boothill.

# MORGAN EARP

Less than five months after the gunfight at the
O.K. Corral, Wyatt Earp had a premonition of
imminent danger. He asked Tombstone resident
Briggs Goodrich if he thought another attempt to
kill the Earps was near. "I think they were
after us last night," Wyatt said.
Goodrich responded that he believed the Earps
"were liable to get it in the neck any time."
That night,

## *March 18, 1882,*

Morgan died during a thunderstorm in a dank
saloon with a bullet hole in his back. He was 31
years old, and his time in Tombstone shed little
light on his brief and violent life.

Most accounts of Morgan's life are sketchy. Those who have attempted to track him prior to his arrival in Tombstone have confronted gaps regarding his whereabouts. The best that can be gleaned from his three decades is a snapshot consisting of impressions, reminiscences, and opinions.

The fourth of the five Earp boys, he was born in Pella, Iowa, on April 24, 1851. At about age 10, when brothers James and Virgil left to fight for the Union in the Civil War, Morgan and younger brother Warren were put to work hoeing the family's corn fields.

He was 13 in 1864 when his father moved the clan to California, and 17 when they packed up again and returned to the Midwest. Morgan appears in 1875 as a 24-year-old process server for Sheriff Charles Bassett in Dodge City, Kansas. Not until the following year did his famous brother, Wyatt, become a Dodge lawman.

While living in that booming cowtown, Morgan met Louisa Houston, a beautiful, Wisconsin-born girl who had moved to Kansas with her sister to work as a "Harvey girl" in the railroad restaurant chain.

Louisa was said to be the granddaughter of famed Texan Sam Houston. According to lore, Louisa's father was illegitimate, born of a union between Houston and a Cherokee woman. There are no records showing that Morgan and Louisa submitted to a legal ceremony either, but they lived together as husband and wife, a common arrangement on the frontier.

Stuart Lake, Wyatt's biographer, picks up Morgan's trail in 1877 in Butte, Montana. Town leaders, thinking they were hiring Wyatt, whose resemblance to Morgan was uncanny, offered the younger Earp the marshal's job.

"When Morgan established his identity," Lake wrote, "Butte decided that if it couldn't have one Earp, it would take another."

Louisa and Morgan were still living in Butte in 1879 when they received word that the Earps were loading their wagons for Tombstone to investigate the big silver strike.

Morgan rolled into the boom-camp on December 8, 1879, a confident young man who liked to drink and was trouble when he did. The man with whom he passed more nights than any other — with the exception of Wyatt, whom he idolized — was Doc Holliday, the trouble-loving, Georgia-born dentist.

"Morgan and Doc were ... carousing buddies," wrote Wyatt's wife, Josephine Sarah Marcus Earp, in her memoir, *I Married Wyatt Earp*. "They had the same tastes and shared the rollicking pursuit of them."

Morgan made a living filling in for Wyatt as a faro dealer at the Oriental Saloon, and when Wyatt quit his job as a Wells Fargo shotgun guard, he arranged to have Morgan replace him.

In addition to physical appearance, the two shared uncommon bravery, and both had great respect among the outlaw class. In the time they worked for Wells Fargo, none of the territory's bandits dared attempt a holdup.

But the brothers were different, too, especially in temperament. Josephine told of a night Morgan stopped by her house in Tombstone for a visit. Wyatt was out of town, and Josephine, who couldn't stand being alone, especially with the feud between the Earps and a gang called the "Cowboys" heating up, invited the young man in.

After supper, Morgan asked if he could sit on the

porch before going home. Josephine agreed and went to bed. A short time later a noise awakened her, and she went outside to investigate.

"Morg was still out there," she wrote, "freezing cold in the winter night, harboring the notion that he was protecting me. ... Morg, you sweet simpleton, get in here this instant!" She set him up with a bed in the small parlor and returned to her room.

Another middle-of-the-night interruption came when Johnny Behan, Cochise County's first sheriff, unexpectedly showed up to evict Josephine, whose house was on a lot held in his name.

Josephine had come to Tombstone in 1880 to marry Behan, but their relationship ended bitterly when she switched her affections to Wyatt. She was arguing with Behan when Morgan charged onto the porch.

"Without saying a word," Josephine wrote, "he hit my former sweetheart in the mouth and knocked him off the porch. When the stunned man got up, Morg hit him in the stomach, doubling him over and causing him to fall again. ... He (Behan) left bleeding from the mouth, but without saying a word.

"The whole episode ... reveals both extremes of Morg's personality, the sweet and the violent."

But the brawl with Behan, a conspirator with the "Cowboys" in their efforts to eliminate the Earps, had a more sinister outcome. When Doc Holliday heard of the fight, he publicly taunted Behan about the whipping he'd received. Josephine believed that humiliation "sealed Morg's fate" and led directly to his death.

Morgan's volcanic nature showed itself again on October 26, 1881. As the Earps walked toward the vacant

lot near the O.K. Corral, Morgan muttered to Holliday, "Let them have it," and the doctor responded, "All right."

"Doc and Morg's responsibility for triggering the bloodshed lay deep in the hothead characters of both men," wrote Josephine Earp. "It may seem strange that such a remark comes out of me. But it is the truth."

When the shooting erupted, Tom McLaury, firing over the saddle of his horse, hit Morgan with a slug that passed through his right shoulder and back.

Holliday saw his friend go down, wheeled on McLaury with a shotgun and practically cut the rustler in two with blasts from both barrels.

At the inquest after the shootout, Virgil and Wyatt lied to protect their hot-headed deputies. Virgil testified that when he ordered the Cowboys to disarm, he heard the ominous click of pistol hammers cocking back, and said,

"Hold! I don't mean that!" Later Virgil swore it was Cowboy pistols he heard preparing to fire. But he knew the clicking came from guns held by his own men.

And Wyatt, hoping to protect his little brother and Holliday, swore under oath that he was the Earp who had fired first.

Despite Wyatt's concern, Morgan insisted on attending a theatrical performance of *Stolen Kisses* at Schieffelin Hall on the night of March 18. A watchful and worried Wyatt accompanied him, and both carried pistols.

After the show, the Earps went to Campbell and Hatch's Saloon on Allen Street to shoot pool. At about 11 p.m., Morgan was standing with his back to a rear door when two shots were fired through its clear glass panes.

The first bullet tore through Morgan's body left of the spinal column. It went on to cause a flesh wound in the thigh of bystander George Berry.

The second shot, intended for Wyatt, slammed into the wall inches above his head.

"Morgan fell to the floor, and was assisted to a lounge in the card room, where he died in less than an hour," wrote Clara Brown, a correspondent for the *San Diego Union*.

"The death scene is said to have been very affecting. The man was surrounded by his brothers and their wives, whose grief was intense. He whispered some words to Wyatt, which have not been given to the public, but spoke aloud only once, when his companions endeavored to raise him to his feet.

" 'Don't, boys, don't,' he said. 'I can't stand it. I've played my last game of pool.' "

Adelia Earp Edwards, Morgan's sister, said that when Louisa heard of the shooting, she "fell down on the floor and sobbed and sobbed."

The identities of Morgan's killers were known within hours. They were a German known only as Freis, woodcutter Florentino Cruz (also called Indian Charley) another half-breed whose name was undetermined, gambler Pete Spence, and Bisbee livery stable owner Frank Stilwell.

Seven months earlier, Wyatt, Morgan and two other lawmen had arrested Spence and Stilwell and accused them of holding up a stagecoach outside Bisbee. As they were being taken into custody, the outlaws vowed to get revenge on the Earp posse.

Morgan's murder touched off a chain of retribution. It began when an enraged Doc Holliday stormed around Tombstone kicking in doors looking for the men he believed were behind the deed.

These included Johnny Behan and Will McLaury, a Fort Worth lawyer and brother of two of the men killed at the O.K. Corral. McLaury aided the legal inquiry that followed the shootout. He was bitterly unhappy when the Earps and Holliday were acquitted.

Two days after the bloodshed in Hatch's saloon, Wyatt was seeing Morgan's body off to California for burial when he encountered Stilwell at the Southern Pacific railroad yard in Tucson. A witness heard the boom of a gunshot, then a man's scream, and more shooting. Stilwell's body was later found riddled with bullets.

"I only ever *had* to kill one man," Wyatt once confided to his nephew. "That was the one that got Morg. I didn't know whether he'd get me or I'd get him, but I knew I had to go after him." Wyatt also ran down and shot Cruz.

The story of Morgan's death carries an eerie postscript. Allie Earp, Virgil's wife, spoke in her memoirs of a remark Morgan made to her on the afternoon of his death.

Gunmen firing from ambush had seriously wounded Virgil three months before, and Morgan commented that he wished Virge would get better, adding, "I'd like to get away from here, tonight!"

# WARREN EARP

Johnny Boyett fired five shots in the
Headquarters Saloon in Willcox. The first four
missed their mark. But the fifth round pierced
Warren Baxter Earp's heart.

It was

*July 6, 1900,*

and Warren became the third of the Earp
brothers to be shot in the aftermath of the
gunfight at the O.K. Corral.
But whether Warren's killing was the final act
of revenge remains speculation.

The gunfight on October 26, 1881, near the O.K. Corral sparked a chain of retributive events. In December, 1881, Virgil Earp, a U.S. deputy marshal at the time, was ambushed and wounded. In March, 1882, Morgan Earp was fatally shot in the back as he played pool in a Tombstone saloon.

Some say the Earps, including Warren, who was not involved in the O.K. Corral incident but was present when Morgan died, set out on a killing spree of revenge. Others believe Wyatt and his posse were acting as peace officers bent on ridding the territory of cattle rustlers.

Whatever their motivation, the Earp posse gunned down at least four men in the months after Morgan's death.

The killing might not have ended there. Although it has never been proven, some speculate that Warren's death 18 years later was the final act in a long revenge play.

The July 11, 1900, issue of the *Arizona Range News* reported that Warren Earp's shooting "grew out of a feud that had existed between Boyett and Warren Earp since the bloody fights between the Earps and Arizona cattle rustlers in Tombstone in the early eighties."

On July 10, 1900, a front-page story in the *San Bernardino Sun* had made the same claim. But the story provided no more details than the headline, which read, "Warren Earp Falls a Victim to a Feud That Had Existed Between Him and His Slayer for Twenty Years."

Although the reason for Warren Earp's killing has never been established, what happened that night is clear. On Wednesday, July 4, 1900, cowboys from the Sierra Bonita and Hot Springs ranches rode into Willcox for a celebration. Among them was Johnny Boyett, foreman at the

Sierra Bonita, and Earp, who worked at the same ranch as an undercover inspector, attempting to curb rustling for the Arizona Cattlemen's Association. Newspaper accounts of the day made it clear that the two didn't get along, and their disagreements came to a head at 1:30 a.m. on Friday the 6th, after a night of drinking.

Eyewitness W. Hayes told the coroner's inquest that he was playing cards in the Headquarters Saloon when Boyett and Earp entered. After the two exchanged words, Earp said to Boyett:

"You was paid $150 at one time to kill me."

"I do not want to have any trouble with you," Boyett replied.

"Go and get your gun," Earp said. "I have got mine."

"I am not afraid of you," Boyett said, then left and walked to the Willcox House, a nearby hotel.

Owner W.R. McComb was in the office when Boyett walked behind the bar and took two guns. McComb demanded to know why Boyett wanted the guns. Boyett replied that he might need them and left before McComb could stop him.

Boyett went back to the Headquarters Saloon and burst through the front door holding two six-guns. According to Hayes, Boyett said, "Where is the s.o.b.?"

Eyewitnesses said Boyett spotted Earp standing 35 to 40 feet away in a doorway connecting the bar to a restaurant. Boyett fired two shots but missed. Earp ducked out through a side door onto the street.

Boyett fired two shots into the floor. Immediately afterward, Earp re-entered the saloon through the side door and began walking toward Boyett.

Eyewitness H. Brown said Earp opened his coat and vest and said: "I have not got any gun. You have a good deal the best of this." In spite of Boyett's warnings to stop, Earp kept advancing. Boyett fired. Earp slumped face forward to the floor. He was dead at age 45.

Sheriff's deputies found no weapon on Earp, except for a half-opened pocket knife clutched in his hand. Earp was buried that Friday afternoon in the Willcox cemetery.

Deputies arrested Boyett, but he was released the following afternoon after a preliminary hearing. The *Range News* reported that Judge W.F. Nichols considered it a "case in which he thought the grand jury would not find an indictment, or if an indictment was found, a trial jury would fail to convict."

But aspects of Earp's murder still puzzle historians.

After his examination of the body, physician M.J. Nicholson told the coroner's jury that Earp was shot in the left side, and the bullet "ranged … obliquely downward."

Some have wondered how Boyett, who stood about 5-foot-6 and was nicknamed "Shorty," could shoot down into a man six feet tall. That has led to theories that Earp was sitting, perhaps playing poker. That speculation contradicts the accounts of the three witnesses.

Investigators also have asked why Earp, who was unarmed, would continue to advance on a man brandishing two pistols. And why were authorities in such a hurry to dispose of the case and Earp's body?

Tombstone historian Ben Traywick asks how Judge Nichols could have known what the grand jury would do. In an article on the killing, Traywick wonders why the district attorney did not attend the hearing or send a representative. Wrote Traywick, "It would appear that this case was already decided before the hearing was held."

Earp's quick burial fueled suspicions that city officials wanted the matter out of the way. On top of that, the grave was unmarked, possibly to make it harder for future investigators to examine the remains.

But the explanation might have been simpler: Willcox residents considered Earp a bully and despised him, so perhaps they felt he didn't deserve a headstone. While few doubt that Earp is buried in the old Willcox cemetery, no one is sure where.

It seems certain that this killing was more than just a drunken encounter between two cowboys.

According to Josephine Earp's account, her husband, Wyatt, called it a clear case of murder, and believed

Warren was only attempting to disarm a dangerous drunk.

In her book, *I Married Wyatt Earp*, she quotes Wyatt as saying: "There had been bad blood between them previously. They called it self-defense. I'm satisfied there was more to it than that. Warren was making it hot for the small ranchers who were rustling to build up herds ... "

Writer Glenn G. Boyer, who compiled Josephine's recollections for her book, noted that while rumors tied the shooting to events in Tombstone 18 years earlier, no connection was made between Boyett and associates or relatives of those shot by the Earps in the early 1880s. Nor have Boyer or others been able to trace Boyett after the shooting.

The *Tucson Daily Citizen* published the following on its front page July 19, 1900: "A great many people in Willcox believed that Wyatt Earp would avenge the killing of his brother, but since he (Boyett) has been killed in Alaska, Johnny Boyett has no cause for further worry on that score."

The *Citizen* provided no details. It is unlikely that Boyett was able to travel from Arizona and Alaska between July 6 and July 19. But the story makes for interesting speculation, however, considering that Wyatt owned a saloon in Nome, Alaska, at the time.

Josephine Earp claimed that after hearing of Warren's death, Wyatt telegraphed Virgil. The two met in Phoenix, then continued on to Willcox to investigate the shooting.

When Wyatt returned to San Francisco, Josephine asked him, "What is going to happen now? Are we just going to let Boyett off?"

"That's about all we can do now," he replied. "The man has disappeared."

Josephine's book says neither Wyatt nor Virgil ever told her what they did in Willcox. But she asked Virgil's wife, Allie.

"You know the Earp boys as well as I do," Allie said with a knowing look. "What happened to Stilwell and Curly Bill and Ringo?"

These were three of the men killed by the Earp brothers in Tombstone in 1882, and Warren was a participant in two of those killings. Allie's remark is perhaps the firmest bit of evidence anyone has found on Boyett's fate.

The youngest of the five Earp brothers, Warren was born March 9, 1855, in Pella, Iowa. Warren did not share in the adventures of his brothers during the 1870s.

In 1877, when his parents returned to the vicinity of San Bernardino, California, where they had lived on and off for years, Warren accompanied them.

There, Boyer says in Josephine Earp's book, Warren operated a small grocery store for his father and is said to have visited Tombstone in 1880 and in early 1881. He returned after the October 1881 O.K. Corral incident and spent the next 10 years wandering the West with older brother Wyatt.

Warren returned to Arizona in 1891. Newspaper accounts state that he worked as a stagecoach driver between Willcox and Fort Grant and later for the Cattlemen's Association. The 1898 Great Register of Cochise County lists him as a bartender in Willcox.

On at least one occasion he had a run-in with the law in Yuma. The incident, recounted in the November 11, 1893, *Arizona Sentinel*, began: "Thursday as Professor Behrens was coming from dinner, he met Warren Earp, who asked him to take a walk across the bridge, which he did. When fairly on the bridge, Earp asked him if he knew what he wanted of him. Behrens said no. Earp said to kill you and throw you into the river, and at that he seized the professor by the neck and endeavored to throw him off the bridge. Behrens being much lighter and rather frail, seized Earp and clung to him so that he could not carry out his purpose."

Earp then offered to let Behrens go and leave town if the professor gave him $100. Behrens bargained Earp down to $25. Behrens promised to deliver the money that night. When Earp arrived to collect his payoff, the professor had him arrested. "I may get two years for this," said Earp to Behrens, "but remember I shall be on your track and will have you yet."

The *Sentinel* reported that Earp had come to Yuma with a woman, who subsequently left him claiming ill treatment. Without providing details, the story said Earp blamed Behrens for her leaving. At his hearing, the charges against Earp were dismissed when he promised to leave town on the next train.

The *Sentinel's* November 18, 1893, issue concluded a second story on Earp's troubles this way: "No man has left Yuma for years that was more pleased to get away. While in jail he was most penitent and said that it was the last time that he would ever get into trouble over a woman."

# BOB PAUL

It sounds implausible, but a case of
stomach cramps played a role in foiling
an attempt to assassinate lawman Bob Paul.
His grit did the rest.
The attempt to kill Paul was made north of
Tombstone about 10 p.m. on

## *March 15, 1881.*

The events of that night typify the life
and character of Bob Paul.

As Kinnear & Company's stagecoach, traveling from Tombstone to Benson, crested a hill 200 yards from Drews Station, a masked man called out, "Hold!" Several more robbers appeared. Shots were fired, and Eli "Budd" Philpot slumped forward in his seat, dead.

"I don't hold for nobody!" Bob Paul hollered. He opened fire with his shotgun, driving off the bandits.

The bullet that got Philpot was meant for Paul, a Wells Fargo shotgun guard whose work had crimped the activities of the "cowboy gang" in southern Arizona. Paul was about to become Pima County sheriff, something the gang knew would further hinder its operations.

So, Paul was marked for assassination. The plan was to rob the stage and shoot the guard, who was supposed to be Paul. But, as the coach was departing Tombstone, driver Philpot complained to Paul of stomach distress, and the two traded places.

"Suffice it that poor Philpot now sleeps peacefully under the daisies," wrote the *Arizona Weekly Star* months later, "and the intended victim, Paul, still lives, sheriff of Pima County, and a dreaded terror to the class of whom his intended murderers formed a part."

Bob Paul's life was marked by numerous such episodes of blood and courage. He was a peace officer who became so familiar in territorial law enforcement that his death in 1901 was front-page copy across the West.

In the ensuing years his name has faded alongside more glamorous figures, such as his friend, Wyatt Earp. But Robert Havlin Paul, a 6-foot-6 inch, 240-pound Irishman, lived a giant life and deserves his place.

He was born in Lowell, Massachusetts, on June 12, 1830. At 14, he became a cabin boy on the Majestic, a whaling ship that sailed east around the world, via Africa's Cape of Good Hope and South America's Cape Horn.

Historian James Barney, writing in *The Sheriff* magazine in 1949, said the Majestic's crew killed 56 whales and produced 3,300 barrels of oil. The boy's share for his first voyage, which lasted 22 months, was $250.

Paul's next ocean adventure nearly cost him his life. His ship was in the northern Pacific, chasing a whale in the fog and rain, when, according to Barney, the whale rammed his boat, breaking Paul's leg below the knee and hurling him into the sea.

"After being in the water one hour and a half - losing blood and the wound tortured by salt water - the boat's crew were rescued by another boat from the ship," wrote Barney. "The young cabin boy's physical endurance at that time was the wonder of the whole ship's crew."

In the ensuing years he sailed to New Zealand, the Sea of Japan, and the Sandwich islands (now called Hawaii). While in the islands he heard of the gold rush in California, and went there in 1849.

But five years in the gold fields yielded little, and in 1854 he began his career in law enforcement. For the next 10 years, in the region of Mokelumne Hill and Camp Seco, Paul served as constable, deputy sheriff and finally sheriff of Calaveras County.

He broke up a notorious gang of outlaws led by Thomas J. Hodges, alias Tom Bell, which had been thieving and killing in the mining district of central California. The prestige Paul gained kept him in the sheriff's office until 1864, when he returned to mining.

But he failed again. In 1874 he went to work for Wells Fargo. In 1878 the company sent him to Arizona to protect bullion shipments from Charleston and Contention City along the San Pedro River to Tucson. Paul did his job so well the *Tombstone Epitaph* called him "one of the bravest and coolest men who ever sat on a box seat."

He needed those skills in the territory — first as a shotgun guard, then Pima County sheriff, detective for Southern Pacific Railroad, and U.S. marshal. The stories of his exploits often involve his trademark shotgun, and his determination to stay on the trail of the outlaws he hunted.

Late in November 1879, Paul set out in pursuit of two Mexican highwaymen who robbed a stagecoach north of Phoenix, killing passenger William Thomas.

"R.H. Paul, Wells Fargo & Co's special detective ... at once was in pursuit of the robbers," reported the *Star*, "and, after following their trail for several days, was frustrated by a storm which entirely obliterated all traces of their course. He has been on the constant outlook ever since."

Three months later, Paul received a tip and chased down one of the robbers, Demetria Dominguez, as he was driving a buggy on the Patagonia road south of Tucson. "Mr. Paul," wrote the *Star*, "deserves great credit for the persevering manner in which he has traced out the whereabouts of this robber and murderer."

In April 1883, Paul, now sheriff of Pima County, used his omnipresent shotgun to halt a mob of angry Tucsonans that had surged into the courthouse to lynch Joseph Casey, who'd coldly shot a Tucson jailer in the back during an escape.

"In an incredibly short space of time," the *Star* reported, "Sheriff Paul arrived at the door of the courthouse, and in a flash he was through the crowd ... and in a twinkling he and his assistants had cleared the hallways."

After Casey's trial, Paul presided at his execution. Standing on the scaffold platform, the condemned man shouted, "Good-bye! Turn her loose!" Paul severed the rope and Casey was gone.

With every outlaw he dispatched, Paul's popularity rose. A stage holdup near Globe in August 1883 put the sheriff on the trail of "Red Jack" Almer and Charles Hensley. On the night of October 3, when the two men showed up at a freighter's wagon near Willcox to buy supplies, Paul and his posse sprang from ambush and called for the fugitives to surrender.

"Trapped, by God!" Red Jack yelled, and began firing.

"The whole posse fired a volley in the dark and the men were heard to fall," Paul told the *Phoenix Weekly Herald*. "Red Jack fell within 20 feet of the wagon. Hensley fell twenty-five yards from the wagon. Then we kept shooting at their flashes."

But Hensley was only wounded. The posse found him the following day, eight miles away. They rode right into his ambush position, and in the opening volley, Paul's horse was shot. But Hensley was quickly killed.

Paul's manhunting reputation grew after three men held up a Southern Pacific train at Stein's Pass, New Mexico, on February 22, 1888. Robbers Dick Hart, Tom Johnson, and Larry Sheehan headed into Mexico with three posses riding hard at their backs.

The first two posses failed and had to turn back. But Paul, a Southern Pacific detective at the time, secured the assistance of Mexican soldiers and tracked the bandits to a ranch house in Chihuahua.

The posse and the soldiers torched the house, forcing a running fight in which the bandits were killed. Paul received national acclaim, and three years later President Harrison named him a U.S. marshal, a position he held until 1893.

Paul was never too quick with his guns. In reminiscences on file at the Arizona Historical Society, J.C. Hancock, a territorial judge and resident of Galeyville, recalls seeing Paul enter a saloon and point his shotgun at Utah murderer Bill Hildreth.

Instead of raising his hands and going easily, Hildreth pulled off his hat and slowly raked his cash and poker chips into it. As the men around him rose and stepped away, Hildreth backed out the rear door of the saloon, leaving Paul holding his shotgun.

Hancock was impressed. "Some officers would have shot Hildreth just to make a name for themselves, but Paul was not that way." On this occasion, he had to figure out another way to get his man.

Paul wasn't without critics. Some allege that in 1884, in his attempt to win a third term as Pima County sheriff, Paul and some friends broke into a safe and changed enough ballots to swing the election away from challenger Matthew Shaw.

And historian Larry Ball, in his book, *The United States Marshals of New Mexico and Arizona Territories, 1846-1912*, reported the conclusion of federal examiners that Paul manipulated the business of his marshal's office to maximize his fees, and he even charged per diems when no business was transacted in the courts.

But Paul's detractors did not include Wyatt Earp. After chasing away the robbers that killed Philpot that night in 1881, Paul struggled for a full mile to halt the racing team of horses.

Then he and Earp formed a posse that chased the robbers over a thousand miles of hard country. They captured Luther King, and from him learned the names of three accomplices.

A year later, in March 1882, the Earp drama that has come to define Tombstone was in full swing. The O.K. Corral shoot-out had occurred the previous October, Morgan Earp had been shot in retaliation, and Wyatt got revenge by gunning down Frank Stilwell at the Southern Pacific Railroad yard in Tucson. The killing resulted in warrants for Wyatt's arrest, and Paul, then Pima County sheriff, was the man to serve them. His friendship with Earp was a secondary concern. Paul's mind, as usual, was on his duty.

But when he reached Benson and met Cochise County Sheriff Johnny Behan, an Earp enemy, Paul would not ride with his posse of "honest ranchmen," which included the likes of Johnny Ringo and Ike Clanton.

"Sheriff Paul ... refused to go after the Earps," reported the *Tombstone Epitaph*, "because the posse selected by Behan was notoriously hostile to the Earps, and said that a meeting with them meant blood, with no probability of arrest."

After fleeing to Colorado, Earp wired Arizona and offered to turn himself in to Paul. "I'll surrender to him any time," Earp said. But the extradition never happened.

**B**ob Paul contracted cancer, and retired from the marshal's office in 1893. The mild-mannered lawman, who loved playing solitaire after supper, died in Tucson on March 26, 1901. He left five children.

The *Arizona Daily Citizen's* obituary captured the story of his life:

"Knowing not fear, never for a moment feeling the impulse of hesitancy when duty confronted him, brave Bob Paul spent the best years of his life protecting the lives, the homes and property of his fellow men, and now that death has claimed him all men will bow their heads — friends and enemies alike — and say: 'He was a brave man and did his duty.' "

# CHAPTER SEVEN

# LAST MANHUNT

In the winter of 1915, Coconino County Sheriff
William G. Dickinson chased murder suspects
Willis and Henry Azbill for seven weeks
through four counties and across hundreds of
miles of hard territory, using wagons,
horses, gas-powered cars, even a boat.
The chase ended for Willis on

*December 25, 1915,*

when the intrepid sheriff swam to the fugitive's
raft and got the drop on him: "Hands up,"
the sheriff ordered.
It was called both the last great manhunt of the
Old West era, and the first of modern time. The
story was covered as far away as Chicago, where
the *Saturday Blade* newspaper described it as "one
of the most thrilling captures in the history
of criminal hunting in Arizona."

In November 1915, cowboys Oak Boggs and Paul Moore discovered a man's body in J.D. Dam, a man-made lake 16 miles southeast of Williams. Secured to the corpse was a gunny sack filled with rocks and tied about the waist by ropes. The skull and arms had been torn loose, probably by coyotes, and were lying on the ground near the torso. The skull was crushed in at least two places.

The victim, who'd been in the water about three weeks, was buried on a nearby hillside. Unidentified, he was perhaps 20 years old, slender, 5-feet-8 with blue eyes, sandy hair, and a fair complexion.

Cattle company manager Nick Perkins said that several weeks before he had discovered two men living in a cabin near the dam. One fit the victim's description. The other was older, roughly clothed, and coarse-looking. He had stooped shoulders, stood about 6-feet-2, and weighed about 180 pounds. The two were riding burros.

The murder weapon, a wrench matted with blood, was found amid a pile of sawdust and rock salt on the floor of the cabin.

Boggs saw the same men, but added an important detail: They were accompanied by a white mongrel dog with a hairless stripe along its back. The older man said the scar was caused by the swipe of a bear's claw.

After word of the murder had spread, a railroad section foreman from Jerome Junction came forward and reported seeing the men riding in two open-top wagons near the dam. The foreman added that the young, sandy-haired fellow was accompanied by two other men who looked remarkably alike. With them was a one-armed woman and a boy of about nine years.

However, the early leads led to blind alleys.

A break came November 20 when Dickinson received a letter from J.P. Strahan, a merchant seeking help locating his friend, missing since early October.

Henry O. Thomas, a 21-year-old Ohio native, had departed Phoenix on a prospecting trip October 9. He was accompanied by a man he'd just met, a fellow Strahan said was a parolee from the state pen.

Magazine coverage of the case states that the man claimed to have a gold mine near Prescott. It was also reported that Thomas was carrying a wad of cash, making robbery the likely motive for his murder.

Strahan came to Flagstaff and said he could make a positive identification by examining the dead man's teeth. "A short time before he left Phoenix," wrote the *Coconino Sun*, "he (Thomas) had complained of a bad tooth and had shown it to Strahan, who advised him to have it extracted."

Strahan and Dickinson traveled to Williams and dug up the body to conduct the gruesome inspection. It was Thomas. The boy's father, C.E. Thomas, of Cleveland, concurred. "The shape of the head, color of the eyes as well as the prominent teeth were identified by the sorrowing father," wrote the *Sun*.

The paper could hardly avoid noting the irony that Thomas came to Arizona every year for his health.

Dickinson's next step was to go Phoenix to search for evidence and retrace the duo's trip north. He traveled to Black Canyon, New River, and Cordes Junction, questioning witnesses along the way. He heard more about the scarred dog and the burros, and he learned that the supposed parolee was squinty-eyed and that the second wagon joined the party somewhere near Cordes.

Dickinson passed through Wickenburg, Mayer,

Humboldt, Prescott, Puntenny, and Jerome. Several times the trail cooled, but another witness would emerge with information, and Dickinson continued tracking.

In Kingman, Dickinson and Mohave County Sheriff Jack Lane learned that the Azbills had sold Thomas' Winchester and his watch at a second-hand store. Farther west, in Oatman, Willis Azbill sold the burros. He was using the name Jasper and apparently had split from his brother, Henry.

The sheriff made an even bigger find when he encountered a Mohave Indian named Nomela to whom Azbill had sold his wagon and a pistol carried by Thomas. Willis, his one-armed wife, and son then crossed to the Needles, California, side of the river.

"The Indian directed me to a place where he was camping," Dickinson testified. "He (Azbill) had built him a boat and started down the river … himself and family."

Fearing his man would disappear, Dickinson got his hands on a rickety, gas-powered launch, and on Christmas morning 1915, the desert lawman shoved off in pursuit.

Sixteen miles down river, he spotted Azbill's wife and son standing on the bank beside their raft. The sheriff anchored his own boat a few hundred yards away and in the company of H.J. Bennett, a cop from Needles, headed through the brush to the Azbill camp.

But Willis was gone. Bennett kept watch while Dickinson searched the area. Before long the sheriff glanced at the river and spotted the Azbill raft, with Willis and family aboard, making a run for it. Dickinson rushed back to his own launch and, unable to find Bennett, took off alone. He shouted for Willis to steer toward the Arizona shore and give himself up.

Willis refused. Instead he ordered his son to disrupt Dickinson's raft by tossing six-foot-long posts into the water. Newspapers accounts describe the boy and his one-armed mother working feverishly to heave the heavy obstacles into the drink.

The logs rammed the sheriff's frail craft, and it capsized. But the dogged, 47-year-old lawman wasn't defeated. He began swimming. Luck intervened when a corner of the Azbill raft hooked on a sandbar and stalled.

"Dickinson placed one hand on the side (of the raft) and a pole came down with cruel force on his fingers," wrote the *Blade*. "He sank below the surface and swam under the raft, and came up on the other side.

"Azbill seized a shotgun and with his wife and boy was watching for the sheriff to come up where he disappeared. The sheriff pulled himself aboard, drew his revolver and ordered 'Hands up!' Azbill then surrendered without further parley and obeyed Dickinson's order to pull for the Arizona shore."

Within days, Dickinson arrested Henry Azbill in Wenden, west of Wickenburg. Acting on a tip, the sheriff sped there in his automobile along battered old wagon roads. It turned out that Henry was the parolee of Strahan's story. He had been released from the state penitentiary at Florence in 1904, after serving four years for a Yavapai County robbery.

Neither Willis nor Henry admitted guilt, and some wondered whether they might succeed at using intimidation to avoid answering for their crime.

Maurice Kildare, a writer who did extensive research on the case, wrote that in the days before the trial began,

Flagstaff filled with toughs claiming to be witnesses on behalf of the brothers. Their intent was to scare County Attorney C.B. Wilson away from prosecution. The matter came to a head one night when Mrs. Wilson and her son, Charles, were walking near a Flagstaff bridge.

"Several roughly dressed men and a woman suddenly leaped out from under the bridge and ran toward them," wrote Kildare. "Grabbing her small son, Mrs. Wilson sped for the nearest lighted home screaming. Her cries brought men from dwellings and the attackers took sudden flight."

But Wilson ignored the intimidation and proceeded. The jury took 15 minutes to return two guilty verdicts. Execution was set for Sept. 29, 1916, but it was postponed because of appeals.

Then fate stepped in on the side of the killers. In November of that year, Arizonans voted to abolish the death penalty, and the following May, Gov. T.E. Campbell commuted their sentences to life in prison. But even that wasn't fulfilled.

On June 18, 1920, the Azbills escaped from Florence. One report states the two brothers "escaped while on their honor and walked away."

Willis was listed as 33 years old at the time. He stood 5-feet-8, weighed 144 pounds, had a mustache, stooped shoulders, and a sober expression. Henry was 40, 5-feet-9, 165 pounds, also slightly stooped in his stance, and he had a circular scar in the center of his forehead.

Those descriptions went out to law enforcement across Arizona. But it was no use. Neither Willis nor Henry Azbill was ever heard from again.

# JIM ROBERTS

The last thing Jim Roberts wanted was fame.
He always turned reporters away, leaving them
to wonder about the oddities of his character,
such as riding a mule instead of a horse,
carrying his pistol in his pocket instead
of a holster, wearing shoes, not boots.
But because of his prowess as a gunfighter,
the man they called the last of the old-time
sheriffs was not to have the anonymity he craved.
He first demonstrated his skill with a gun on

## August 10, 1887,

in what became known as the
Pleasant Valley War. He shot five men
in a battle below the Mogollon Rim. Fame
followed him from then on.

James Franklin Roberts came to Arizona as a teen-ager. He built a cabin at the head of Tonto Creek, eventually putting together enough money to raise and breed horses.

But the land on which Roberts settled eventually would explode into the Graham-Tewksbury feud, which lasted two years and left more than 20 dead. Roberts took up guns against the Graham family after his horses were rustled and his cabin torched.

On that fateful August day in 1887 on the Middleton Ranch below the Mogollon Rim, the Tewksburys and Grahams battled it out. Jim is said to have killed Tom Paine with his first shot, and knocked Hampton Blevins out of the saddle with his second. He turned his weapon on Tom Tucker, another Graham man, sending a bullet through his lungs, then wounded two more.

"In less time than it takes to tell it," one magazine wrote, "two cowmen had been killed and three wounded, attesting to the accurate shooting of Jim Roberts."

The incident resulted in a murder indictment against Roberts and several others on the Tewksbury side. But the charge was dismissed, and Roberts emerged from the war with a reputation as a brave and proficient gunman.

Yavapai County Sheriff William "Buckey" O'Neill was so impressed that he appointed Roberts as his deputy. "I want the best gun on my side," O'Neill explained.

Roberts' career in law enforcement began with a stint in the mining community of Congress. At a dance there he met Permelia Kirkland, a 20-year-old blonde called the belle of the town. A profile of Roberts in *Reader's Digest* in 1950 described the young peace officer, wearing a black bow tie and high-buttoned suit, showing up at Permelia's door two days later. She was so impressed with her eager suitor that she tossed her fiancee aside. "He was a nice boy," Permelia recalled many years later. "But he wasn't the man Jim was." They were married in November 1891.

That same year Roberts was reassigned to Jerome, a copper camp on the slope of Mingus Mountain where saloons howled around the clock with hard men, easy women, and trouble. The *New York Sun* called it the "wickedest" town in the nation.

Roberts put himself in the middle of the turmoil. In May 1895, he saved the life of prisoner Jose Soto, under arrest for breaking into the room of a waitress at the Grand View Hotel. When rumors circulated that Soto's intention was rape, an angry mob set out to lynch him.

"Soto's yell and the prompt arrival of Sheriff Roberts frustrated all plans that were intended to have been carried out against Soto," reported the *Jerome Chronicle*.

Rooming house operator George Ward also owed Roberts his life. Ward set a trap to capture the man who had been burglarizing his establishment, and ended up killing the masked intruder with a shotgun blast. Chums of the dead man, part of a colony of Italian miners, hollered murder, and threatened Ward's life. In his book, *They Came to Jerome*, writer Herbert Young said Roberts confronted ten of the men as they departed their friend's funeral.

"You fellows have been asking who gave Ward the authority to take the law into his own hands and kill a man," Roberts said. "Though it's none of your business, I'll tell you. I gave him the gun and told him to shoot anyone who tried to rob his place or molest him at any time."

Roberts warned the men to back off or deal with him. The threats ended but Jerome continued to roar, especially on nights after the United Verde Copper Company dispensed its payroll. Without a jail, Roberts stashed prisoners anywhere he could. *Reader's Digest* wrote that on some nights it looked as if Roberts had "half the population handcuffed — to posts, wagon wheels and wagons."

It took more than handcuffs to tame bad men Dud Crocker and Sid Chew, who rampaged one night and killed a blacksmith's helper and Roberts' deputy, Joe Hawkins.

After being roused from bed, Roberts threw a saddle on his favorite white mule and, leading a pack animal, rode out of town after the killers. In *Ghosts of Cleopatra Hill*, historian Young wrote that he crept up on their camp on the Verde River the next morning.

"No need of shootin'," Roberts called through the early sunlight. "Just drop your guns. Don't draw."

Crocker and Chew jumped to their feet, separated, and began firing. Young's account has Roberts dropping Crocker with a single shot in the head, and Chew making a charge that ended just as quickly. Young wrote that Roberts rode into town that afternoon with the two killers draped over his pack mule. He delivered the bodies to the undertaker and wired Prescott to send him a new deputy.

Roberts' work earned him wide acclaim. *The Arizona Republican*, a Phoenix paper, said order finally had been restored to Jerome.

"This may be … accounted for by the efficient work of the marshal, Jim Roberts, who is very popular in the camp, but will not tolerate any lawlessness," the *Republican* wrote. "He is a fearless man, though generous and whole-souled."

But bravery could not ward off personal tragedy. In a three-week period in 1902, he lost three of his children to scarlet fever. Two years later he and Permelia left Jerome

and stayed away more than 20 years, living in Douglas, Florence, and Humboldt.

In 1927, Roberts returned to the area as a deputy sheriff in Clarkdale. Those who remembered him from his Jerome days found it sad that the 71-year-old was spending most of his time tilted back in a chair outside Miller's store, chewing tobacco, whittling, and occasionally directing traffic. It was largely a ceremonial position for the old lawman, known to most as Uncle Jim.

Roberts rejected an opportunity to profit from past adventures when a Hollywood crew came to Clarkdale to film Zane Grey's novel about the Pleasant Valley War, *To the Last Man.* Roberts was asked to be technical director. Some wrote that the job would've paid more money than Roberts had ever made. But Jim said he had promised never to discuss the events of 1887 and 1888.

As for Grey's novel, few doubted that the true identity of the last man was Jim Roberts himself.

The old lawman still had a round in his single-action Colt. At 11 a.m. on June 21, 1928, two bandits burst into Clarkdale's Bank of Arizona and ordered the manager to stuff their gunny sack with cash. David O. Saunders turned over about $50,000, and robbers Willard Forrester and Earl Nelson fled in a stolen Chrysler touring car.

Roberts happened along. He drew his weapon and shot once at the fast-moving car. The bullet hit Forrester in the back of the head, killing him instantly.

The car crashed into a school building. Nelson jumped out and emptied his gun at Roberts. One bullet nicked Gus Schneider, a telegraph operator, knocking the watch from his pocket. Nelson tossed his gun, and bolted, but Roberts captured him before he had made 200 yards.

Years later, Permelia recalled that her husband was late coming home for lunch that afternoon. "Jim said he was sorry," she remembered, "but he'd had a little trouble."

The incident put Uncle Jim on front pages. "Now at 72, his eye is still keen and his actions with a six-gun are as vivid as the dart of a rattlesnake," wrote *The Arizona Republican*.

Roberts' reaction was typically muted. After receiving a citation from the governor, he told the *Verde Copper News*, "Well, weren't nothing wonderful about it. Forrester just got in my way."

Six years later, on January 8, 1934, Uncle Jim was making his nightly rounds when his heart gave out. He was found on the ground behind the Clarkdale drugstore. He died in an ambulance en route to the hospital.

His headstone in Clarkdale's Valley View cemetery, in the shadow of Mingus Mountain, reads simply — Roberts.

# CHAPTER NINE

# WOMAN KILLER

Constable Marian T. Alexander
violated the strictest prohibition known
in the West — he killed a woman.
His deed, on

*February 7, 1901,*

was considered so ghastly
that nothing short of his corpse
could set things right.

Alexander, the constable of Somerton, set out for a ranch 11 miles south of Yuma. He was accompanied by Frank Miller, who was embroiled in an ownership dispute with the ranch's occupants. Miller sought to evict Joseph and Mary Burns and their children. Alexander reportedly had gone to the ranch earlier to evict them and was confronted by Mrs. Burns toting a rifle. He backed down then.

But this time Alexander brought his shotgun. Also with him and Miller was William Fain. The *Arizona Daily Star* for February 10, 1901, reported:

"When the men arrived, Mrs. Burns was some distance from the house, and evidently had anticipated trouble, as she had a Winchester rifle in her hands. Alexander told the other men to remain where they were and he would go over and settle the difficulty with Mrs. Burns. He rode up to within a few feet of the lady and alighted from his horse.

"A quarrel ensued during which Alexander became enraged, and taking a double-barreled shotgun from a scabbard on his saddle, deliberately fired both barrels at Mrs. Burns, the shot taking effect in the abdomen."

Mary Burns fell dead in a field in front of her children.

News of the killing raced across the territory by wire, and the reaction was chilling. Even before a full account was available, Alexander was judged a murderer. He must have heard the calls for his head, because that night he turned himself in, asking to be locked up in the Yuma Territorial Prison where a lynch mob couldn't get to him.

Alexander's surrender didn't silence those who sought to demonize him. The loudest voices came from the territorial press.

*The Arizona Republican* wrote that few facts were

known, except that "a man murdered a woman," and "the county jail was not deemed strong enough to save the murderer from the indignation of the citizens."

A harsher tone was set in a *Republican* editorial on February 9. It noted the finding of the coroner's jury — that the killing was "not entirely excusable but under mitigating circumstances" — and said:

"The photographs of the gentlemen who composed this remarkable jury would, no doubt, be highly prized by those persons engaged in the business of collecting curiosities. The details of the tragedy are not now obtainable, but we can conceive of no 'circumstances' in which the killing of a woman could have even the color of an excuse."

After noting that Yumans were threatening to make "a ghost of this slayer of women," the editorial concluded with this: "We believe that this constable will wish some time that instead of returning to Yuma after the slaughter and giving himself up, he had gone to the banks of the Colorado and buried himself in its yellow flood."

Yuma's streets and saloons filled with rumors. One involved Frank King, Mary Burns' brother. He reportedly was heart-broken at his big sister's death and on his way from Tucson to Yuma.

The Kings were a widely-known pioneer family with a reputation for taking care of their own. The *Republican* described them as a "peaceable" lot, but said that "when provoked they do not estimate human life highly."

Frank King was quoted in one press account as denouncing the killer for not having "the humanity to take the body into the house," but allowing it to lie in the open for seven hours before neighbors removed it.

In a letter to the *Republican*, King praised the paper's incendiary editorial as having "the right ring," and added:

"Too many irresponsible no-account men are elected to our minor offices in Arizona, and most of the tragedies in official performances are enacted by 'cheap' fellows who have been given these small offices."

But Frank King, cattle broker, former owner of Nogales' *Border Vidette* newspaper and one-time undersheriff of Maricopa County, didn't come to Yuma alone. He was accompanied by his brother Samuel, a former line rider for U.S. Customs, and the family's hot-headed patriarch, Sam Houston King. They made it known that only the death penalty for Alexander would satisfy them. It was as if a clock had begun ticking on his life.

William Fain must have heard the ticking. On February 13 he escaped the policemen protecting him. The first group to ride in pursuit consisted of the King brothers and Joseph Burns. They rode south from Yuma along the Colorado River. Sheriff Guy Livingston's posse followed. Neither group found Fain.

Eleven days later Fain turned himself in, saying he would rather face the law than the Kings' vengeful guns.

A grand jury indicted Alexander, Miller, and Fain on March 25. But according to Yuma author Bernts Rube, writing for the National Association and Center for Outlaw and Lawman History, it was hardly unbiased. Among those on the jury was the victim's brother, Samuel. How such a conflict of interest could occur has never been explained.

But it probably didn't matter. Public opinion was so strong against the suspects, especially Alexander, that neither the grand jury, nor the trial jury, could have gone against it. The only support for Alexander, a good-looking,

24-year-old Texan, came from some women who packed the courtroom daily. One of them proclaimed that she would give four months' salary to see the defendant set free.

The judge told jurors that if Mary Burns had a gun then Alexander had a right to arrest and disarm her, and, according to Rube, "that right was in no way diminished by the fact the deceased happened to be a woman." But on April 9 the jury found Alexander guilty, and he was sentenced to life in prison.

After Alexander left the Yuma County Courthouse under police guard, a sniper shot him. He collapsed near the railroad tracks at Third and Madison Streets with a gaping hole in his back.

Livingston and his deputies drew their guns and hurried to the house from which the shot came. They saw Samuel King running from the scene. A few minutes later, they found his father nearby. Both were arrested.

The rifle shot had set off pandemonium in the courthouse. The murder case against Miller had just begun, and the excitement forced Judge Webster Street to adjourn. The rush to get outside was so great the glass in the courthouse doors was shattered.

But Street didn't stop at adjournment. According to Rube, he hopped a train and didn't find out until he got to Phoenix whether Alexander had survived.

He didn't. The rifle slug tore through his liver and bowels, and he died at the city hospital at 10 p.m., several hours after the district attorney had ordered Sam Houston King and his son released. Neither man was armed at the time of his arrest, and no witness came forward to identify either as the shooter. The only case that could be made against them was circumstantial.

**M**iller and Fain were luckier. The shooting of Alexander convinced authorities to move their trials. Fears were high that they too would be killed.

Late in May, after allowing tempers to cool for seven weeks, Livingston spirited the two men out of Yuma on a midnight train to Yavapai County.

Lawmen there, determined not to allow a repeat of the Yuma incident, reportedly warned the Kings not to show up in Prescott. The only familiar figure in the court-room was Joseph Burns. The case against Miller went to trial in June, and he was acquitted. The charge against Fain was dismissed a month later. Prosecutors had little evidence against either man.

The conclusion of legal action in Yavapai County did not end the whispers about the Kings, and whether they had made their own justice. Rube reported that old-timers in Yuma said a rifle was later found in a bale of hay near where Sam King was taken into custody. But if true, no one in law enforcement did anything about it.

Years later in *Wranglin' the Past*, Frank King's frontier memories, he said that Alexander was seeking "a reputation as a bad gunman." King also wrote that family friends had sent telegrams offering to help, some with guns and some with money, after hearing of Mary's death. "But it turned out that we did not need any help other than what we had — the whole citizenry of Yuma County," King wrote.

In another part of his memoirs, King admitted:

"It has always been the custom of our family," he wrote, "to kill anyone who kills any member of the family."

# BURT MOSSMAN

As foreman of the Hashknife, an outfit that ran 60,000 head of cattle in northern Arizona, Burton C. Mossman accomplished what the law could not. He stopped the rustling that nearly ran the ranch broke in the 1890s. That feat made him territorial Governor Nathan Oakes Murphy's choice in 1901 to run the newly formed Arizona Rangers. Mossman held the job for only a year, but built a reputation as a captain who ran the Rangers with swagger and dash. In the final days of his appointment Mossman pulled a grand coup that defined his leadership of the Rangers. On

## *September 4, 1902*

Mossman brashly rode into Mexico and the camp of Augustino Chacón, a renegade said to have killed more than 50 people. Mossman captured the desperado with a daring ruse.

Mossman had persuaded a couple of outlaw friends of Chacón to reveal the killer's location in exchange for immunity. With one of the outlaws, Mossman crossed the border at Naco, south of Bisbee, and at daybreak rode up to Chacon's campfire. Chacón's friend said Mossman had broken out of jail north of the border.

Mossman asked Chacón for a cigarette. Chacón warily handed over tobacco. Mossman plucked a stick from the fire and lit his cigarette. Then he dropped the burning stick as if it had singed his hand, and he started rubbing the hand against his leg. Now his hand was near his holster, and in an instant he jerked his gun and had the drop on Chacón.

It didn't matter to the persistent Mossman that he made the capture four days after his commission had expired. After all, he had no authority in Mexico, with or without an Arizona Ranger's badge. Besides, the Rangers and their Mexican counterparts, the Rurales, had an informal understanding that each could cross the border into the other's territory in hot pursuit of criminals.

Mossman took Chacón back across the border on horseback, flagged down a train, and deposited him at the jail in Benson. From there, the killer was returned to Solomonville, where he had escaped the day before he was to be hanged, having cut a bar with a hacksaw while his girl friend kept the jailer occupied with amours.

From the gallows, Chacón looked at the crowd and said: "Adios, todos amigos" — goodbye, all my friends.

# CHAPTER ELEVEN

# MICKEY FREE

The 12-year-old boy was tending
stock on a ranch in southern Arizona
when Apache warriors swooped down,
stole 20 head of cattle, and took him with them.
Thrust into a new life
on that fateful day,

## January 27, 1861,

he lived as an Apache and learned
to track, shoot, hunt, and kill.
Wrongly blamed for the abduction, Apache Chief
Cochise started a campaign of destruction
that lasted more than a decade.
The boy became an Army scout known as
Mickey Free. His friend, Al Sieber, the famed
chief of scouts, described Mickey as "half-Irish,
half-Mexican, half-Apache and whole sonof-
abitch." He meant it as praise.

Mickey Free was born Felix Martinez about 1848 in Santa Cruz, Mexico. His mother was Jesus Martinez, and his father was a light-skinned, blue-eyed man, probably of Irish descent, named Tellez.

In 1858, after Tellez's death, Jesus moved with her children into the Sonoita area of southern Arizona and took up with — though never married — a prosperous farmer named John Ward.

After the abduction, Lt. George Bascom led a command out of Fort Buchanan and tracked the renegades to Apache Pass. On February 4, 1864, Bascom met the Chiricahua Chief Cochise at the Overland Mail station. What followed is known as the Bascom affair, a much-analyzed incident in which the inexperienced officer brashly, and wrongly, accused Cochise of taking the boy. The result was a standoff, then shooting.

Cochise, bitter at what he considered a betrayal, vowed never to let a white man look upon his face again and live.

John Ward and Jesus Martinez never saw Felix again. They died about 1867 believing the boy was dead. But according to author Allan Radbourne, who studied Free's life for the *English Westerners' Brand Book*, the boy was handed over to the San Carlos Apaches, who raised him.

"Felix Ward came into contact with a whole new way of life," wrote Radbourne, "and effectively disappeared from the pages of recorded history for over a decade, to eventually emerge as Mickey Free."

How Felix Ward got the name Mickey Free is unknown. One theory is that a bad pronunciation of his Apache name sounded like Mickey Free.

In his years with the San Carlos, Mickey learned to track, shoot, hunt, and kill. He signed on as a scout at Fort

Verde in December 1872. Army records listed him as 5-feet-7 and 135 pounds. His pay was $20 a month. He was to be present at almost every incident of the Apache conflict, from the Battle of Big Dry Wash to the escape of the Apache Kid, and the pursuit of the renegade Victorio.

At first, Sieber neither trusted nor liked Free. But a bloody incident in Mogollon country in 1875 changed that.

Cavalrymen were herding some Apaches from Camp Verde to San Carlos when a snowstorm struck. In the confusion, a horse stumbled into a ravine and broke its neck, and one of its riders, a nine-year-old Yavapai Apache boy, broke his leg. Sieber pulled the boy onto the back of his horse and the group went on.

"They were hardly started when Sieber felt a sharp pain in his back," wrote A. Kinney Griffith, whose extensive writings on Free's life include a biography. "As he jerked around he felt the pain lessen and saw his own Bowie knife flash in the boy's hand for another stab."

But Free killed the boy with a knife. He shot the boy's mother in the head as she lunged at Sieber with a saber. "Twice in the space of a few breaths," wrote Griffith, "Mickey Free had saved Al Sieber's life."

From then on Sieber trusted Free, and relied on him.

Once Sieber assigned Free to capture an Apache who had murdered a cavalry corporal and fled San Carlos. After tracking him for 300 miles, Free caught the renegade and slashed his throat. But the body was too heavy to haul to the reservation, and Free needed proof of his kill. So he carved out the renegade's face, and wrapped it in the dead man's jacket. He dropped the rotting trophy at Sieber's feet. For his work Free got a good meal and a bottle of whiskey.

Many of the stories told about Free hint of romance, if not outright fiction. Sieber said he "could track a shadow on a rainy night," and in his autobiography, Horn called Free "the wildest dare-devil in the world," a man with fiery red hair, a small red mustache, and "a mug that looked like the map of Ireland."

A more common description was "ugly." Free's left eye was a gray blob cocked at an odd angle, the result of a cataract he developed as an infant. He let his stringy, unkempt hair fall over his face to hide it.

In his history of Arizona published in 1916, J.H. McClintock wrote that Free was "about as worthless a biped as could be imagined, ugly, dirty, unreliable and dishonest." McClintock was echoing Charles T. Connell, who worked with Free at San Carlos in 1880 and described him as a "wandering half-breed whose being caused the woeful events of a decade."

Although it was false, the half-breed label stuck, and contributed to the view that Free was less than human. But the Army valued primitivness in its scouts.

"The nearer an Indian approaches a savage state," wrote Gen. George Crook, who chased Geronimo without success, "the more likely he will prove valuable as a soldier."

Geronimo reviled Free. In May 1885, when the Indian leader broke from captivity at the San Carlos Reservation, Free dogged him relentlessly. He once tracked the Apache chief and his renegade band 200 miles south from the reservation into Mexico.

When Geronimo sat down with General Crook for a peace conference in March 1886, he used his opening remarks to launch a tirade against Free. Geronimo considered Free a liar and scoundrel, and said he fled San Carlos because Free was plotting to kill him.

He might have been right. But to the Army, Free was invaluable. In July 1886, he was chosen to join Chiricahuas who traveled to Washington to lobby for better treatment.

It's a difficult sight to imagine: Free, a wild man meeting with polished bureaucrats, hobnobbing with reporters eager for his translation of various meetings, even shaking hands with President Grover Cleveland.

On its return trip to Arizona, the Chiricahua delegation, including Free and other scouts, was arrested and sent to Fort Marion, Florida. More than any other event, this betrayal highlighted the enigma of Free's life. He had done what the Army asked of him. Yet he was tossed into the stockade with Chiricahuas he had once pursued.

After being released, Free returned to Arizona, and in May 1887 re-enlisted as a scout. It was the only life he knew, and by then he had become a swashbuckling celebrity.

He liked wearing his hair in twin braids, with his blue military uniform, cavalry boots reaching above his knees, and a belt around his waist holding two big dragoon pistols. But fame made Mickey no less vicious.

"When your correspondent saw him (Free) his head was in bandages, as he had been badly hurt a few days before while making a murderous assault upon a sergeant of the garrison," wrote a reporter for the St. Louis *Globe-Democrat* in 1890.

After calling him "the worst man on the reservation," the writer said Free and "his squaw were drunk and made an unexpected attack upon the soldier, but he, being a powerful fellow, succeeded in throwing them off and saved himself by knocking them down with the butt of his gun."

Free quit the scouts in July 1893. Ten years later Horn wrote that Free was living on the Fort Apache Reservation with "a large Indian family, and is wealthy in horses, cattle, squaws and dogs, as he himself puts it." Free married four times and fathered four children.

In his last years, Free was bent over, losing vision in his right eye, and racked by tuberculosis. But according to Prescott writer Kenneth Calhoun's manuscript on file at the Arizona Historical Society, the cunning tracker had one job left in him.

About 20 miles from Free's tin shack, another retired Apache scout and his son-in-law were shot dead when they confronted two cowboys butchering one of their cattle. The old manhunter, hobbled by illness and near death, got his rifle and his knife and rode out.

In a few days he returned to Fort Apache leading two riderless horses. Free sold the mounts, along with their saddles and bridles, and gave the money to the widow. But he kept the cowboys' guns and boots for himself.

A short time later, on December 31, 1915, Free was found dead in his shack with a Catholic missal in his hands. It was the final contradiction in the life of a man who took his pay, killed his master's enemies, and survived.

# CHAPTER TWELVE

# TOMBSTONE'S LAST HANGING

Tombstone's real-life Wild West theater staged its final act, a public demonstration of revenge masquerading as justice on

## November 16, 1900.

Thomas and William Halderman, convicted of murdering two lawmen, were hanged before an approving throng.

The Halderman brothers kept their nerve on the scaffold. Their coolness probably had a simple explanation: Innocent men needn't fear the judgment of their maker.

Thomas, 18, had never fired a shot, and his big brother, William, 21, probably had been acting in self-defense when a deputy opened fire on them.

Violence erupted in April 1899 after rancher Buck Smith swore out a warrant accusing the Haldermans of shooting some of his cattle. Constable C.L. Ainsworth of Pearce rode toward the Chiricahua Mountain ranch of J.N. Wilson, where the Texas-born brothers were staying. Along the way, Ainsworth stopped at a ranch and asked 18-year-old Ted Moore to help with the arrests.

The Haldermans obeyed Ainsworth's call to step outside and listen to a reading of the arrest warrant. The boys gave no sign of resisting, so Ainsworth relaxed his guard. He asked if they'd had breakfast. They hadn't, so he said they could eat before leaving for Pearce. The Haldermans disappeared inside the ranch house.

Wilson would testify later that he was at the corral saddling a mule when he heard Tom Halderman shout, "Hands up!" Then came gunshots. Wilson saw Tom standing in one doorway, William in another. Both were armed.

The *Tombstone Epitaph* reported that one of the first shots hit Ainsworth below the left eye, knocking him out of the saddle and killing him.

Wilson attributed at least eight shots to the Haldermans. The last one, fired when the fleeing Moore was 150 yards away, pierced his back. Wilson said that before the brothers fled, he heard William say, "We got one of (them) and the other cannot go far. Dead men tell no tales." Moore rode 12 miles to his family ranch and collapsed in front of his mother. He died four hours after being shot.

A posse led by Sheriff Scott White and Deputy Sid Mullen captured the Haldermans near Lordsburg, New Mexico, on April 16.

Talk of lynching started on the morning of the killings

and intensified when the brothers were dumped into the iron tanks of the Cochise County jail. The *Tombstone Prospector* led the charge, saying "a little stretch of hemp would have a wholesome effect," and demanding that there be "no legal quibbles bringing long delays and opportunities of escape from any punishment ...."

The boys' prospects grew bleaker with news that the prosecution would be led by C.F. Ainsworth, the territory's attorney general and brother of the slain constable. The *Prospector* described this conflict of interest as a "touching spectacle of brother seeking to avenge brother."

The trial began June 17. The prosecution opened with an emotional wallop, bringing Moore's mother to the stand to recount the story Ted told before he died at her feet.

Wilson testified on what he saw from the corral, and concluded with the "dead men tell no tales" remark that he attributed to William Halderman. "This testimony was regarded as a clincher," wrote the *Prospector*.

Attempts by the defense to create reasonable doubt failed, although Wilson's daughter, Mary, admitted that he had urged her "to testify nothing favorable to the prisoners, and if asked who had fired the first shot, to say the prisoners did."

Rena, another Wilson daughter, said she heard Moore and William Halderman arguing, and Moore threatening to kill him. That supported the Haldermans' contention that they acted in self-defense. They said that when they retreated into the house, William told Thomas they had better fetch their guns in case Moore tried to make good on his threat.

Thomas said he returned to the door, gun in hand, to explain to Moore the brothers' intention to ride armed.

Thomas claimed he shouted "Hold up!" not "Hands up!" and was reaching for his hat when Moore began shooting.

William said he fired a few rounds from one doorway, then ran to Thomas' side, wrenched the rifle out of his brother's hands, and continued firing from there. William corroborated Thomas' testimony that he never fired a shot.

As for Ainsworth's death, William said the constable was shot accidentally, perhaps by Moore, and he denied saying anything about dead men not telling tales.

The jury was handed the case at 10 p.m. June 19, and at the start of court next morning they declared the boys guilty. The sentence, death by hanging, was to be carried out August 25, 1899.

The executions were delayed three times over 15 months. The territorial Supreme Court denied the defense request for a new trial, and a new death date of August 10, 1900, was set.

The boys were spared again on August 9, when President William McKinley, responding to the pleas of influential Texans, ordered a stay of execution.

Then in mid-September 1900, with the third death date three weeks off, territorial Governor N.O. Murphy stepped into the maelstrom, making what Tombstone author Ben T. Traywick described as a theatrical trip to the county seat to review the case. Murphy was running for Congress, and his opponent was Marcus A. Smith, one of the Haldermans' defense lawyers. The governor postponed the execution again. But Smith still defeated him handily.

Meanwhile, defense lawyers amassed evidence, and what they discovered should have overturned the verdict, or at least brought a new trial.

They found a juror who allegedly boasted that he'd

"starve the jury until the Haldermans were hung." And they got Mary and Rena Wilson to state in affidavits that the Haldermans were not the first to fire, and that their father had warned them not to testify about this or they wouldn't have "a friend in the county."

The defense also submitted a statement by Buck Smith, who withdrew his charge against the brothers, and said later evidence revealed Ted Moore had shot his cattle. In reporting this revelation, the *Epitaph* wrote that Moore evidently had killed the cattle "for the purpose of throwing blame upon the Haldermans, with the elder of whom, William Halderman, he was at enmity."

But none of this swayed the court.

On April 8, three train robbers broke out of the jail in Tombstone. They shot Deputy George Bravin and opened cell doors to allow other prisoners to flee. But the Haldermans stayed and tended to Bravin's wounds.

Instead of acknowledging that it had exaggerated in portraying the boys as beasts, the *Prospector* wrote that most assumed it was "a shrewd attempt to divert public sympathy in their favor."

Even the plight of Thomas couldn't silence the death drums. He wrote to Governor Murphy, pleading for justice:

"Honorable Sir, I did not shoot one single shot, did not take the life of either of the men. ... But still my life is demanded. Oh, sir, I'm not afraid to die. I can walk to the scaffold and go to meet my dear parents knowing I am innocent."

On the morning of the hanging, William told the *Arizona Daily Citizen*, "I could go out there and die as easy as water runs in the river if it was not for Tom going by my side. That's what sticks me."

As the Haldermans entered the gallows yard, the eyes of 100 people were fixed on them. Others watched from the courthouse windows. The spectators included seven jurors.

Those near the scaffold later described the Haldermans as clear-eyed and brave as the nooses were fastened — one by George Bravin. What was in Bravin's mind as he helped execute the men who, instead of fleeing to freedom, sought to comfort him as he bled? And what were the thoughts of the jurors who watched the fulfillment of their judgment? Surely, by then, they harbored doubts.

None of the accounts say how many of the seven looked away at 12:38 p.m. when the gallows doors swung open.

# MASS LYNCHING

Vowing to eliminate unruly elements from their
town, 23 armed men left their homes in
Flagstaff in the wee hours. Down Whiskey Row
the vigilantes marched, taking men
from saloons, gambling dens, back alleys,
and flop houses.
One outlaw was shaving in his rooming house
when he was hauled away. Another sat in the
parlor of a bordello sipping a beer with his
prostitute. One man, half-dressed and barefoot,
dived through a window and escaped.
But nine others met their fate in the
predawn darkness of

*August 28, 1885.*

With their hands bound at their backs, the
nine were taken to a pine tree on the edge
of town and lynched from the same stout
branch. They remained there, a sight beyond
imagination, for almost 24 hours.

The work of the vigilantes became Flagstaff's blackest secret, one kept for almost 44 years. Even the town newspaper, the *Arizona Weekly Champion*, failed to take notice of nine bodies swinging in the wind.

On April 5, 1929, the first testimony was heard. That came in a letter to *The Coconino Sun* by C.L. Christensen, an Arizona pioneer living in Moab, Utah.

Thirty-seven years later, the story came to the attention of northern Arizona writer Gladwell Richardson, who set out to unravel the secret. With the sons and daughters of town pioneers as his sources, Richardson published a portion of the story in the June 1966 issue of *Southwesterner* magazine, under the name Maurice Kildare, and a longer version in *Zane Grey Western* in 1974.

Bear in mind that Richardson was a pulp writer with a flair for inventiveness, especially in writing tales of lost gold. Many believe his claims on that subject existed as much in his mind as reality. But his work on the hanging has a different, reportorial feel. He lists names, places, times, and a wealth of other detail on a subject that received scant mention in history books, memoirs, and diaries.

Flagstaff was booming in 1885. Construction of the Atlantic and Pacific Railroad transformed a sleepy settlement into a bustling town packed with lumberjacks, cowboys, track graders, and bridge builders. Saloons rumbled around the clock on a new Whiskey Row, located along what became Route 66. Hookers soon came to town, and so did knife-packing drifters and "derringer boys." Robberies and pistol-whippings totaled up to a dozen a night.

The *Champion* called for the law to act. But the sheriff's office for Flagstaff, then part of Yavapai County, was 87 miles away in Prescott. Prominent citizens, such as

Johnny Berry, owner of the San Juan Sample and Club Room, believed only private guns could bring public peace.

When a ruffian accused Berry of running crooked gambling and threatened to dynamite his saloon, Berry wrote to the *Champion* and promised to protect his property, even if it meant fitting the threat-maker for a coffin.

Some months later the *Champion* warned: "Our citizens should be on their guard, as there is a hard winter coming and desperate characters are laying around waiting for opportunity to steal and murder for a few dollars."

But the situation worsened. On June 13, 1885, the *Champion* published this warning: "Flagstaff is at present afflicted with a number of cutthroats, some of whom are wanted for crime elsewhere, ostensibly 'tinhorn' gamblers by profession who ought to be ordered out of town ...."

When the criminals did not heel, Berry and five other saloon owners, mindful of threats made by robbery victims to torch the town, met secretly to plot action. The conspirators were led by J.J. "Sandy" Donahue, owner of the Mineral Belt Saloon, and included Andy Munn of Our Boys Saloon, D.A. Murphy of the Phoenix, Cal David of the Keg, and James A. Vail of the Palace Exchange.

To identify the riffraff to eliminate, they hired rancher Thomas F. McMillen, a teetotaler unknown in the saloons, to go undercover. With gold coins furnished by the saloon men clinking in his pocket, McMillen headed for Whiskey Row and made himself a target for the tinhorns.

He hit paydirt his first night when two thieves stuck a gun in his belly outside the Keg Saloon, then slugged him. Richardson described McMillen sinking to the wooden sidewalk in mock distress, all the while recording a mental description of the robbers.

"He studied the pair as they walked away unhurriedly, meeting a third, well dressed man two doors along the street. Fairly good light from a saloon front window shone full on the man whose identity astonished him.

"The suave, handsomely slender individual was the gambler who ran the poker table in Vail's Palace Exchange. Known only as Joe ... he was well-liked and deemed an honest gambler."

McMillen's four nights on Whiskey Row, each in a different disguise, yielded a list that was presented to the saloon men and 20 of their lieutenants in early August. They voted to send the troublemakers an ultimatum. Several mornings later, a hand-lettered placard was found tacked to every door on Whiskey Row: "Notice — Tinhorns have 24 hours left."

Richardson noted that a few thieves and floaters left town. But the worst of them stayed. Ten names were picked from the list. At 3 a.m. on the 28th, under bright August stars, the vigilantes went to work. Vail insisted on capturing gambler Joe himself, and used a ruse to summon his employee to the Palace Exchange. As Joe entered, four pistols were fixed on his gut. "Well, well, so I'm your huckleberry, gentlemen," the gambler sneered.

The hangings went off without accusation or ceremony. The only victim to speak was gambler Joe. "This indeed takes me by surprise," he cracked, then the nooses were tossed over the branch and the loose ends tugged down until feet dangled in the air.

Dawn must have been an acute horror for C.L. Christensen. He was leading four freight wagons into Flagstaff when he spotted the hanging tree. He turned back. When he went into town later that morning, the bodies were still there. Richardson's research revealed that whispers coursed through the streets, but there was no uproar. A few citizens rushed to the hanging tree to look. But they were turned back by stern-faced men who insisted there was nothing to see.

Cowboy Pete Brogdon hitched a wagon and, with the help of the sheriff's deputy and the town marshal, cut the nine men down. Brogdon buried three of the corpses himself, without caskets in unmarked graves. He was paid $2.50 per man.

Sheriff Billy Mulvernon hurried in from Prescott, but no one would answer his questions, or even admit knowing of a hanging. Whiskey Row was empty. The remaining tinhorns had jumped trains and freight wagons, or simply walked out of Flagstaff — anything to escape the noose.

"As time went on," Richardson wrote, "people believed that the identity of those who took the law into their own hands would come out. But it didn't, and far from being dissolved, the lid of dead silence whammed on even tighter."

Even Christensen's letter was muted. He described seeing the bodies, and very briefly recounted a story told him by an unidentified man — about the rash of holdups and McMillen's role in uncovering the perpetrators.

"I have written nothing but the truth as understood then," Christensen wrote. "I do not wish to intimate that Mr. McMillen did any unlawful act in the vengeance on the outlaws. I do not pretend to know who did, or that anyone did."

Richardson told of his efforts to coax more details from Christensen. But Christensen never penned another word about what he saw or heard. Nor did his companion that day, Tuba City resident Harmon Zufelt.

The daring Tom McMillen returned to ranching life, his undercover role known only to his wife and the six saloon men. Sandy Donahue later became sheriff of Coconino County and Jim Vail became prosperous running his Palace Exchange Saloon.

But Johnny Berry's fate was ironic and far less rosy. A year and a half after the vigilante action, he was shot dead in a saloon scuffle. A few days later a mob forced its way into the Flagstaff jail and murdered the two brothers who were suspects in Berry's killing, thus keeping the wheel of vengeance spinning.

As for the nine hanging victims, they remain unidentified. Perhaps their most significant recognition came in *Flagstaff Whoa*, the memoirs of pioneer George Hochderffer, published in 1965.

"As the years have been passing by," wrote Hochderffer, who lived within sight of the hanging tree and the nine mound graves, "I have seen these mounds gradually overrun with grass and wild flowers and sunk level so that not a vestige or trace can be found of where they had once been."

The burial site, at the base of Observatory Hill, is today a park. The old cemetery was moved about 1910, but none of the unmarked graves was disturbed. The hanging tree was chopped down many years later.

It's a pretty spot for picnics, tennis, and lazy afternoons in the mountain sun. Just pay no mind to the nine tinhorns still resting there, strangled in the dead of night in the cause of lawfulness by men without badges.

# CHAPTER FOURTEEN

# CATALINA KID

Four shots were fired in the Palace Saloon and four men fell, each with a bullet in his head. Less than two hours later, Nogales awoke to find downtown gutters running with blood. The carnage took place on

## January 27, 1905.

But the destiny of the four men had been determined less than a week earlier when one of them, a saloon keeper known for his honesty, fired a young card dealer he thought was cheating.

Sensational though it was, the shooting also is remembered for another aspect — the characters involved. The most vivid Hollywood imagination would be hard-pressed to produce a cast such as this:

M.M. Conn, the Palace's beloved owner. He was a huge, square-shouldered man, nicknamed "Daddy." He instructed his employees to collect money left on the bar by patrons so it could be returned to them the next night. Conn was so honest it wound up killing him.

Ferdinand Walters, nicknamed the "Catalina Kid." A gambler with an outlaw past, he wore a Dracula-like black cape and reportedly was partial to opium.

Irene Wells, a buxom saloon entertainer with long, red hair. Practically topless, she sobbed uncontrollably over the body of her boss.

There were more than two dozen witnesses to the shooting and its aftermath, but each told a different tale of the Palace Saloon massacre.

In one crucial respect, the shooting didn't happen as reported. The Catalina Kid did not end the carnage by killing himself. He was shot by the Palace's hired gun, Dave Black, whose name for 50 years was absent from public discussion of the incident.

The Territorial Legislature's ban on gambling was still four years away when the Missouri-born Conn opened his saloon in July 1903. In his first two years of operation, the burly entrepreneur achieved a reputation for straight dealing. When suspicion grew that his dealer was using "papers," or marked cards, in his stud poker game, Conn quickly fired him.

The 28-year-old Walters had been living in Nogales

only two weeks, but rumors flew. Some said that in 1897 he had been a member of "Soapy" Smith's notorious gang of confidence men and bandits headquartered in Skagway, Alaska, and that he had committed crimes in Dawson, Nome, and over the California coast. The rumor was strong that he was an opium smoker.

Walters wasn't at his job long before those around him noticed he was set off by the slightest "wrong word" or backward glance. One Nogales newspaper, the *Oasis*, described Walters as "an extremely sensitive individual and appears to have made much of apparently trifling grievances."

He took great offense at his firing by Conn, then had to endure relentless needling from J.J. "Cowboy" Johnson, his replacement at the stud table. By Thursday, January 26, less than a week after his firing, the Catalina Kid had endured about all he could take.

In the Monte Carlo saloon, he was overheard promising to produce "a few dead men by sunrise." At the time, he was playing stud poker, and according to the *Oasis*, "played in bad luck all night, losing nearly $100." Just before 4 a.m. Friday, perhaps under the influence of opium, he walked down Morley Avenue to the Palace. The details of what happened next vary in the lengthy stories in the *Oasis* and the *Nogales News*. But from the two it's possible to cobble together this probable sequence of events:

Wearing a black mackintosh coat, with a long, red-lined cape, the Catalina Kid strode into the Palace and ordered food. After eating, he ordered a ham sandwich, which he stuffed into his coat pocket.

Rising from his chair, the Kid stepped toward Johnson at the bar, jerked a Colt .45 from his coat, and fired once from less than four feet. The bullet struck Johnson between the eyes. "His victim fell in his tracks," the *Oasis* reported, "but breathed some time before the spark fled."

At the sound of the shot, Conn sprang from his seat near the monte table and bolted for the door. The Kid turned toward him and fired once. The round passed through Conn's head, made a clean, silver-dollar-sized hole in the Palace's glass door, and shattered the show window of the Escalada Brothers' Store. The 56-year-old Conn dropped to the floor, his "fetish for honesty," as one friend called it, rewarded with a bullet behind the ear.

The Kid next turned to a rancher-turned-card-dealer named George Spindle. Just as the Kid fired, Spindle swiped the gun aside with his hand. So close was the Colt that the charge left powder stains on his face, and a hole in the brim of his hat. Spindle dropped to the floor and played dead.

Modesto Olivas, a father of five and one of Conn's monte dealers, was not so fortunate. The bullet meant for Spindle hit Olivas in the head.

The Kid then stepped over Conn and walked out to Morley Avenue. In the *Oasis'* account, the Kid "placed the muzzle of his smoking revolver to his own head, and with a single shot ended his earthly existence."

The *News* came closer to the truth: "David Black, as soon as the shooting began, ran for his revolver, and seeing it, darted out through the doors after the murderer. Before he could raise his weapon, Walters placed the Colt against his own head and fired."

Nogales resident Jess Marleau arrived within minutes. His recollections are in the Artisan Leslie Peck, Sr. collection at the Arizona Historical Society. Peck was a Nogales pioneer, who, along with his family, chronicled events along the border over several decades.

"I wanted to see who was killed," Marleau said, "so I pushed the swing-door in, and hit Conn in the head with the door. Conn was a great big fellow and he was groaning."

Marleau saw Spindle dashing up the street, "scared to death, and breathing hard." And he saw Irene Wells, "a very good-looking red-haired woman." Marleau remembered that Wells, "her beautiful hair all loose and flying, and her low-necked dress pulled down so that her bare breasts were hanging," was leaning over Conn. "Shoot me, too!" she screamed. "Shoot me, too!"

Asked by the sheriff to retrieve the Kid's gun, Marleau slipped a hand under the fallen man's chest, and the Kid "started coughing and blood shot out of his mouth."

Marleau never found the Colt. It might have yielded evidence that the Kid had fired only three times, and therefore could not have killed himself. As it was, the matter was whispered about for years by witnesses quietly certain of what they saw — Black pursued the Kid and when he spun to shoot, Black fired first.

The question of how the Kid died wasn't discussed publicly until 1956, when old-time Nogales resident Billy Bower stated that Black had taken the Kid down.

"I know Dave Black killed him," said Bower in Peck's papers. "I saw him pull the gun out of a drawer ... Everybody in there said no (that Black did not kill him). But I saw him shoot. They didn't want to get Dave in trouble. (I) can see that man (Black) like it was today."

As if to remind Nogales of what it wished to forget, Modesto Olivas' blind son, Chico, spent his fatherless years playing his fiddle in a destitute neighborhood called the Street of Rags. No one could hear Chico's brilliant fiddle without thinking of the night his father was murdered.

Little is known of Irene Wells' fate. In Peck's papers it's mentioned that she entered into a death-bed marriage with a Texas gambler mentioned only as Raymond.

Three years after killing the Kid, Black suffered a mental breakdown and was taken to the Territorial Insane Asylum. What became of him after that is not recorded.

After the territory banned gambling in 1907, the Palace's new owners brought in a series of novelty acts, among them Professor Dupuy and his boxing cats. Nogales greeted their appearances with yawning indifference. Eventually the saloon closed.

# BRONCO BILL

Although he was on the run,
"Bronco Bill" couldn't stay away
from the dance in Geronimo, Arizona.
While cohorts stood guard, Bill went from
one woman to the next, asking:
"May I have the honor of this dance?"
They all said no, whereupon
Bill began shooting at their feet,
sending the women and their beaus
scrambling for safety.
It was

*July 4, 1898,*

the day on which
the bandit's undoing began.

At 5-feet-9 and 135 pounds, he was hardly an imposing man. He spoke softly, had bright blue eyes, a firm jaw, and the tanned skin of a ranch hand. His nickname, a testimony to his skills on a horse, was "Bronco Bill." His given name was William Walters. Many who knew him said he was a happy-go-lucky cowboy.

But some wondered about his ever-present smile. No matter how tense the situation, the grin was always there, wide and empty.

Bronco Bill's first appearance at the Diamond A ranch in southern New Mexico in the 1880s aroused the curiosity of ranch manager Walter Birchfield, but he hired the lad, who had showed up on foot, having walked across the border from old Mexico.

As Birchfield would learn, that was Bronco Bill's way. He was a shadow, dark, out of nowhere and without a past, an angry wind who for two decades whipped across Arizona and New Mexico, eventually becoming one of the most wanted train robbers and murderers of his day.

Bill's reign of terror occurred mostly in New Mexico, where he eluded the posses that snapped at his heels. But when matters became too hot, he crossed into Arizona, and used the rugged White Mountains as his hideaway. This was a mistake. A group of tough Arizona lawmen eventually brought Bill to heel in a gunfight at Black River.

But another factor helped bring this mysterious man to justice, a character trait that had to do with his favorite pastime: dancing. Bronco Bill Walters, feared outlaw, who, according to one friend, could "shoot running jackrabbits with his six-shooter from a fast-moving Model T Ford," loved to take women in his arms and let the music carry him away.

**B**ill's criminal career did not begin in grand style. His idea of a big heist was to swipe a few horses, or use his six-guns in a stickup. One such incident occurred October 16, 1890, in Separ, New Mexico, south of Lordsburg. Bill and Mike McGinnis, another crooked cowboy, shot up a boarding house in an attempt to relieve a miner of the $480 he had stashed in a sack.

The plan went awry when the miner, half-dressed and scared to death, ran off into the darkness, taking the sack with him. Bill and his partner responded by turning their pistols on the town, blasting away at anything that caught their fancy.

With help from Lordsburg, local authorities arrested the two and hauled them to jail in Silver City. Five months later Bill got a gun and escaped, establishing a pattern that would be repeated several times during his career. It seemed that no matter what jail he landed in — from the lockup at Socorro to the state prison at Santa Fe — the shadowy Bronco Bill soon was scrambling over the wall.

After the Silver City escape in February 1891, Bill fled to Las Palomas, Mexico, where for the first time his fondness for dancing would lead to his capture.

Grant County Sheriff J.A. Lockhart deputized Cipriano Baca and sent him to Las Palomas with orders to gain Bill's confidence and lure him back into New Mexico, where he could be arrested.

The *Silver City Enterprise* described the deputy's plan: "Baca knew the fugitive's weakness and proposed to give a dance and stand the whole expense if Bronco would get the music. (Bill) fell in with the idea, and as the matter was discussed over a long bottle of Mexican spirits, visions of Mexican señoritas gaily tripping to the inspiring music of the violin floated before Bronco's uncertain vision."

Bill tumbled for the idea of returning to New Mexico to secure a violin. There, Baca made his identity known, and Bill was wearing handcuffs.

The Separ shooting earned Bronco Bill a term at the penitentiary in Santa Fe, and it prompted the *Enterprise* to write: "He has shown a disposition to become a bad man, but a year's reflection in the pen may change his determination."

It did, but in the wrong direction. In the years after his release, the outlaw's tastes turned to train robbery.

On March 30, 1898, Bill and his gang — including "Kid" Johnson and Daniel "Red" Pipkin — robbed the Santa Fe Pacific train at Grants, New Mexico. The Denver *Evening Post* reported that the robbers opened fire on the train as it approached the depot, shattering windows and wounding fireman Judson Lathrop. Railroad employees C.C. Lord and Charles H. Fowler returned the fire, driving the outlaws away under a rain of bullets.

Two months later Bill's bandits robbed a train near Belen, 30 miles south of Albuquerque. The outlaws commandeered the express car and dynamited the safe, scattering booty in every direction. One source states that Bronco Bill marveled at how "paper money came floating down out of the sky like snow." The take was reported to be $20,000.

Pursuit of the gang was a lethal venture. Peace officer Francisco X. Vigil, his deputy Dan Bustamente, and two Indian trackers caught up with Bill and Johnson on Alamosa Creek, southwest of Belen. Pipkin had apparently gone off on his own. The bandits were still in camp when Vigil approached to within 40 yards and demanded their

surrender. Bill and the "Kid" jumped up, threw their hands in the air, and jawed with the posse. All the while the two were inching toward their rifles.

The gambit worked. In the ensuing gunplay, Vigil, Bustamente, and one of the trackers were killed. Vigil and the tracker reportedly were felled by single shots to the head, which some cite as evidence of Bill's stunning marksmanship.

Now the chase was really on, and Bill seemed to enjoy it. After easily eluding several New Mexico posses, he headed for the White Mountains of eastern Arizona.

Then, hearing that U.S. Deputy Marshal Jeff D. Milton was leading the effort to capture him, Bill sent the former

Texas Ranger a message. It was a taunt for Milton to come and get Bill, and to bring plenty of good horses and warm blankets because he'd need them.

Milton gladly took up the challenge. Riding with George A. Scarborough, a detective for the Grants County Cattlemen's Association, Milton headed for Holbrook, Arizona, to await the bragging train robber.

Bill showed up on July 4, 1898, at a schoolhouse in Geronimo, Arizona. A dance was being held there, and Bronco Bill couldn't stay away.

According to one published account of the incident, Johnson and Pipkin stood guard at the schoolhouse door while Bill approached a row of young women seated with their escorts in front of some open windows. He went from one to the next, asking: "May I have the honor of this dance?" They all turned him down, whereupon Bill began pumping bullets into the floor at their feet. The women and their escorts bolted from their chairs and dove out the open window.

The Geronimo dance might have been Bronco Bill's idea of a night out, but it proved to be his undoing. Milton, aware now of his quarry's general whereabouts, plotted a trap.

Operating on the theory that Bill, a cowboy at heart, would seek the company of other cowboys, Milton, Scarborough, and two other men rode into Joseph Hampton's Double Circle ranch camp on the Black River southwest of Springerville.

In a 1936 interview in the *Arizona Daily Star*, Milton said he ordered the arrest of everyone in the camp: "We were taking no chances that one of them would pass the word to Bill that we were in that part of the country. We camped back of the corrals and took turns in watching."

On July 29, 1898, the three bandits appeared on the trail a quarter mile from camp. Johnson and Pipkin stayed back to shoot at rattlesnakes, while Bronco Bill cantered down to the corral.

What happened next is in dispute. Some accounts say that Milton confronted Bill. Other evidence indicates that after Bill dismounted, he spotted Scarborough and said, "I guess I don't want to be here," then quickly remounted.

"Hold on there, Cap," said Scarborough. "I want to speak to you."

Bill went for his pistol, and the firing began.

"He shot to kill but he was so excited, and his horse was traveling so fast that most of the shots went between my legs," remembered Milton. "We shot at him several times before we hit him. Then he stiffened straight out in his saddle and fell to the ground."

Using Winchester rifles, Milton and Scarborough next took aim at Bill's confederates, still up on the trail.

Pipkin's horse was shot from under him, and Johnson was hit by a slug that passed through both hips and his lower intestines. Fatally wounded, Johnson reportedly called out, "It's no use, Red. I can't go. Save yourself."

Pipkin disappeared into the hills, but later was captured and sent to the Yuma penitentiary.

With the guns silent, Milton grabbed Bronco Bill by the ankles and dragged him to the ranch. He thought the outlaw was dead, but learned otherwise when he saw blood gush from Bill's mouth. A doctor later told Milton that jarring Bill's body expelled blood from his lungs and probably saved his life.

Milton sent a terse message to Fort Apache that since has become a Western classic: "Send two coffins and a doctor. Jeff."

Bill was sentenced to life at the Santa Fe pen, but on April 16, 1911, The *Fort Sumner Review* wrote:

"Bronco Bill, noted murderer, train robber, crack shot, former cowboy of Grant County and desperado, with a more thrilling history than Diamond Dick or some of the other heroes of the dime novel library, and whose face has the half amused smile 'that won't come off,' made his escape from the penitentiary some time Sunday night and in a thoroughly thrilling manner, worthy of the man and his career."

Bill was captured three days later. In an interview with the Albuquerque *Evening Tribune*, he explained why he quit the lam so easily: "I will never use another gun as long as I live. I have killed in my time. I will never kill another man. I could have fought my way out of New Mexico, but I have quit the bad game for good."

This undoubtedly prompted guffaws among *Tribune* readers, but it proved true. Bill was pardoned in 1917 and returned to work as a cowboy at the Diamond A, the same ranch he joined when he walked up from Mexico more than 30 years before.

He died at the ranch on June 16, 1921. Bronco Bill Walters, the cowboy-killer who twice surrendered his freedom because he loved to dance, was repairing a windmill when a gust of wind blew him to the ground, breaking his neck.

# THREE-FINGERED JACK

The differences between
"Three-Fingered" Jack Dunlap and Jeff Milton
are hard to overstate.
Milton was an open book, his life the subject
of newspaper coverage so extensive it made him
famous throughout the West. He was a hero.
Dunlap was an enduring mystery.
His age, birthplace, and the manner
in which he acquired his memorable nickname
are all unknown. Even his real name is in doubt.
If opposites attract, then the meeting of these
two was pre-ordained. The face-off came
at tiny Fairbank, Arizona, on

*February 15, 1900.*

The long road to the face-off commenced in Nogales on August 6, 1896. Riding with William T. "Black Jack" Christian, Dunlap and three other men — Jess Williams, Bob Hayes, and George Muskgraves — attempted a midday robbery of the International Bank.

The *Oasis* newspaper reported that Williams and Hayes entered the bank, "thrust a pair of cocked navy revolvers" toward cashier Fred Herrera, and ordered him to raise his hands. Herrera complied while inching cautiously forward. "That movement brought him within a step of the counter, underneath which, on a shelf, lay a loaded, self-cocking revolver," reported the *Oasis*.

Bank President John Dessart made a panicked run for the front door. As he went by, one of the robbers "leveled a vicious blow to his head, inflicting a scalp wound which bled profusely."

Seeing some $10,000 on the pay desk, one of the robbers moved to scoop it up. In doing so, he passed the open door of a room occupied by five men. The robber leveled his pistol at them, ordered them to sit tight, and closed the door. This distraction allowed cashier Herrera to make his move. "Instantly he seized his revolver, raised it and fired at the man in front, who incontinently ran through the front door," wrote the *Oasis*.

Herrera turned to the other man, who was fleeing out the back door. The cashier fired and the robber fell, dropping the money bag. Then he rose, clutching his knee, although it was never determined whether the shot hit him. He circled to the front of the bank, where a cohort helped him onto a horse. The five men galloped off empty-handed.

"They did not get the value of a Mexican five-cent piece," according to the *Oasis*.

Posses from Nogales, Bisbee, and Tucson chased the gang into southeastern Arizona's Chiricahua Mountains and across the San Simon Valley. According to author J. Evetts Haley, Dunlap and Christian were liked in the area and were able to change horses at virtually any ranch.

"They would ride until their horses grew weary," wrote Haley, "round up a fresh bunch wherever they were, unerringly catch the best, and sweep on across that great and wild terrain ahead of all who hunted them."

Christian's gang, dubbed the "High Fives" after a card game then in vogue, went on a crime spree after the Nogales bank job.

The gang attempted to rob a train in Rio Puerco, New Mexico, and held up D.W. Wickersham's store and post office in Bowie, Arizona. A week later the outlaws raided the settlement of San Simon. Then they robbed the Huachuca Siding railroad depot west of Tombstone. Lawmen killed two of the High Fives in these actions. In April 1897, lawmen gunned down Black Jack Christian near Clifton, Arizona.

Whether Three-Fingered Jack rode with the gang after Nogales is unclear. Published accounts of the spree do not mention him. But he could have been with the High Fives, using an alias.

He used enough aliases to fill a hotel register. He was known as Jack, Jess, or Jesse. In his book *Tombstone's Yesterday*, Lorenzo Walters wrote that Jack was born John Patterson. The *Coconino Sun*, in noting his July 1894 arrest near Tuba City for cattle rustling, called him John Dunlap.

Toughness was a trademark of Jefferson Davis Milton. He became a Texas Ranger at 19, and by 23 he was a deputy sheriff in Socorro County, New Mexico. By the time he moved to Arizona, Milton had won considerable renown as the chief of police who cleaned up El Paso, Texas.

At the time of the robbery Milton was a highly regarded Wells Fargo messenger. He joined a posse chasing the gang. Although several posse members quit the hunt, Milton wasn't about to fold. Christian's death ended the work of the High Fives, but it didn't change Milton's intent on catching Three-Fingered Jack.

Several magazine writers have claimed that Jack was just as intent on getting Milton, an intent the outlaw announced to anyone who would listen. Writer J.S. Qualey claimed that over the next few years Jack twice took shots at the Wells Fargo man.

"One bullet wounded Milton, but Milton kept on the

trail," Qualey wrote. "Three times he had the outlaw cornered, but each time Three-fingers (sic) Dunlap slipped out of the trap."

The inevitable and climactic confrontation came at Fairbank on February 15, 1900, when the New Mexico & Arizona train stopped at the town's railroad depot about dusk. Milton was unloading packages to agents on the platform when he heard a voice calling for hands up. He thought it was a joke by cowboys greeting the train. But when he looked up, Milton saw Three-Fingered Jack, the man he'd been hunting since the summer of 1896.

"Milton made a rush for his Winchester, and as he did so the robber fired, the shot striking the messenger in the forearm, staggering him against the car," wrote the *Arizona Daily Citizen*. "Milton did not lose his head, but stood guard against the invasion of the robbers, firing when the robbers came within the scope of his vision."

In a 1936 Associated Press story, Milton told a slightly different version. When he saw the bandit, he tossed the keys to the safe into a far corner of the car, grabbed his shotgun and put a charge into Dunlap's belly. It was at this point, Milton recalled, that Dunlap shot him in the arm.

"I managed to get the door shut, and, grabbing the sleeve of my shirt, tore it up to the shoulder and was able to twist it enough to stop some of the blood," Milton recalled. "It was spurting out in a stream and covering my face and clothes. Then I fainted."

Milton collapsed between two trunks. The five robbers shot a fusillade of bullets into the car, but the trunks saved him. Using a railroad employee as a shield, the robbers entered the car. Milton passed out again.

"I felt myself going," Milton recalled. "But I enjoyed

it. I heard the most beautiful music, the most wonderful band I ever heard in my life. I wonder if every man does."

The thieves never found the keys and made off with only $17 in Mexican money.

The train was backed up to Benson where a special car took Milton to Tucson. A surgeon at St. Mary's Hospital removed fragments of bone from Milton's arm. He avoided amputation, according to one published story, by drawing a pistol from under his pillow and threatening to ventilate the doctor.

Milton recovered and resumed his career. He died in Tucson in 1947, at age 85. Obituaries quoted Milton as saying he "never killed a man that didn't deserve killing."

The public's fascination with Milton's bravery was matched by its revulsion at the treatment Jack received. After he fell from his saddle, his gang abandoned him in the desert, gut-shot and in agony. Fourteen hours later, a posse found him, unable to move. He was taken to a Tombstone hospital. He had three wounds in the groin. A fourth bullet, inflicting the most serious wound, had entered at the abdomen and passed through his liver.

The *Prospector* tossed a tip-of-the-hat to the outlaw, writing that he "bore up with remarkable fortitude."

Before he died, Jack named the other gang members: brothers George and Louis Owens, Bob Brown, and a man called Bravo Juan. All were captured within a few days.

"I am too weak to talk," he told a *Prospector* reporter. "I'm getting weaker all the time. I guess it's all up this time."

Jack died seven days after the Fairbank incident. He was buried at Tombstone's Boothill cemetery.

# BLACK JACK KETCHUM

"My advice to the boys of the county
is not to steal horses and sheep,
but either rob a train or a bank
when you have got to be an outlaw,
and every man who
comes in your way kill him.
Spare him no mercy,
for he will show you none."
That advice was proffered brashly
by "Black Jack" Ketchum on

*April 26, 1901,*

and then they hanged him.

Two strangers rode into Camp Verde about eight that night. They tethered their horses at a corral adjacent to a weathered adobe building that once housed soldiers during the Indian Wars. The building was now a general store. One of its owners, R.M. "Mac" Rodgers, was sitting on the porch enjoying a peaceful evening of conversation with retired Army Capt. John Boyd, part-time clerk Lou Turner, and Dick Hopkins, the mail carrier between Camp Verde and Payson.

One of the strangers ambled up to the porch and chatted with the four men for about 20 minutes. No one viewing the scene could have guessed that what was about to occur would be described as the Verde Valley's most atrocious and cold-blooded crime.

The violence erupted when the stranger arose with a six-gun in his grip. He commanded Rodgers to move inside. Instead of complying, the frightened merchant bolted toward a room where he kept his gun.

"Stop, Mac, that won't do," commanded the stranger. Then he put a round into the back of Rodgers' neck. The *Prescott Journal-Miner* reported that the 36-year-old store-keeper was dead before he hit the floor.

Rodgers' business partner, Clint Wingfield, was working at his desk in the back of the store when he heard the shot. He would explain later that he thought the report was a firecracker. But he started out to investigate anyway.

The stranger doubled around to a back door, came up behind Wingfield, and shot him in the back. He would survive, in great pain, for two more hours.

Then, the stranger confronted the other three men on the porch. "I might as well kill you all," he reportedly said as the men scattered.

Boyd, a cripple, couldn't move fast enough and got a bullet in the thigh. Turner and Hopkins ran as fast as they could, somehow avoiding the gunman's aim.

The killer met his accomplice at the corral, and they galloped away in the direction of the Tonto Basin. Sheriff Johnny Munds of Prescott and Deputy Joe Drew rounded up a posse that included Indian trackers, and they set off in pursuit.

The case of the Camp Verde murders was a strange one from the start, and it stayed that way to its macabre conclusion. That took place 21 months later when the notorious outlaw Thomas E. "Black Jack" Ketchum was hanged in Clayton, New Mexico.

But Ketchum's capture and execution didn't answer the central question of this terrible episode: What motive did he have for shooting two store owners?

Some have speculated that Black Jack went to Camp

Verde to satisfy a grudge carried from Texas, where Rodgers and Ketchum grew up. But no good cause was ever given for that theory.

Robbery seemed a possibility, too, although Ketchum made no effort to steal anything. He could have done so easily without killing.

But brutality was Black Jack's way. Even though he was about to be hanged, he wrote his criminal philosophy on a slip of paper, and his "advice to the boys of the county" has survived through the years as a chilling reminder of a soul-less man.

Ketchum lived his twisted philosophy. He was born in 1863 in San Saba County, Texas. By his 21st birthday he was rustling cattle with his older brother, Sam. By 1897, the Ketchum boys were the leaders of a feared gang of train robbers that included Dave Atkins, Will Carver, and William Ellsworth "Elzy" Lay.

Their careers spanned only two years, during which they pulled five confirmed jobs in Texas and New Mexico. But Black Jack didn't confine his activities to those states.

As the *Arizona Daily Citizen* for April 26, 1901, noted: "Every Cowboy in the San Simon country, on the Blue, and in the Sulphur Springs Valley has at some time or other run across Black Jack." Those encounters often ended badly for the other party.

The same article told the story of a shooting at the Triangle Ranch in Arizona's Eagle Creek country. The foreman of the ranch, a man named Noble, had gained Black Jack's enmity. One night, Ketchum, accompanied by a member of his gang, rode up to the ranch "heavily armed, spurred and booted."

Dad Richards, the ranch cook, recalled that after

shaking hands and engaging in polite conversation, Noble and Black Jack went into a room. Then Richards heard two shots. Noble was dead, and Richards made the mistake of confronting Black Jack. He suffered a flesh wound on the right side and a hole in his arm. He got away with his life by turning over a table, dousing the lamp that had been on top of it, and running outside to hide in the weeds.

Such cowardly deeds made Black Jack a hated man. One account refers to him as a supreme loser among gunfighters of the West, a man lacking in style and class.

Even his nickname was the result of a mistake. Writers of the day confused him with another outlaw-robber named "Black Jack" Christian. After Christian's death the name was wrongly applied to Ketchum.

The hunt for the Camp Verde killer proved frustrating. Munds followed the few leads he had to Payson, where his questioning turned up the name of Charley Bishop, a drifter who had been camping on the Mogollon Rim all summer. He hadn't caused any suspicion until he came to town and purchased ammunition for his pistol and his rifle.

Munds learned that Bishop now was holed up in the mountains above town. Before long, the posse found his abandoned camp.

But what Munds didn't yet know was that the man he was chasing was Black Jack Ketchum, who was accustomed to living with the law at his back. Black Jack led his pursuers on a wild chase, sometimes obscuring his tracks by padding his horse's hooves and riding in among herds of sheep.

One day the posse found another of the outlaw's camp sites and a taunting note scrawled in pencil: "Boys, I know you are after me. I'll be back in two or three hours and if not, I'll be four miles north gathering bees."

Months later, a lawman asked Bishop, who by then had been identified as Black Jack Ketchum, why he left the note. The outlaw responded:

"Oh hell, I thought I'd like to have 'em know which way I'd gone, so when I left the place where I camped that night, I wrote a few lines on a cracker box for whoever might find it."

The posse quit its futile expedition after deciding the quarry had fled into New Mexico. But a determined Munds went after him, hopping a train to Albuquerque, where he learned of the arrest of a man who had tried to stick up a train near Clayton, New Mexico, on August 16, 1899.

Ketchum, for reasons that remain unclear, had been without his gang on this robbery. He boarded the Colorado and Southern train in Folsom (the town had been named after President Cleveland's wife, Frances Folsom) and hid in the coal tender. Four miles outside town, he crawled into the cab and ordered the train stopped.

When mail clerk Fred Bartlett stuck his head out the door to have a look, Black Jack fired a warning shot that ricocheted off the side of the car and struck Bartlett in the jaw.

Conductor Frank Harrington grabbed a shotgun and cracked open the door to the platform just enough to get the barrel out and trained on Ketchum. Two blasts sounded almost simultaneously, one from Harrington and the other from Ketchum. Harrington was grazed in the neck, and Black Jack's right arm was nearly shorn off by buckshot.

Ketchum jumped from the car and fled into the brush.

He was arrested the next morning sitting near the tracks waving his pistol in the air. It had a white handkerchief attached to the barrel.

Believing that the Camp Verde assassin and the Folsom train robber were one and the same, Munds went to Santa Fe to interrogate the prisoner. Black Jack admitted nothing. Munds showed pictures of Ketchum to Captain Boyd, who was at the Camp Verde store when the killings took place. Boyd made a positive identification.

But Munds' efforts to have Black Jack extradited to Arizona were thwarted by New Mexico's governor, Miguel Otero, who felt that the prisoner, suffering badly from blood poisoning caused by the shotgun wound, would not survive the trip. On September 3, 1899, Ketchum's right arm was amputated.

He was found guilty of train robbery and — under a New Mexico statue that made train robbery a capital offense — sentenced to hang. The execution was carried out on April 26, 1901, outside the Clayton jail.

Black Jack kept his cocky composure throughout most of the day. Only once in the long morning of waiting did his temper crack.

"Why don't they hurry?" he barked. "I'd like to eat dinner in hell."

After refusing the attentions of a priest and mounting the steps to the gallows platform, he was met by executioner Salome Garcia, who'd braced himself for the deed by loading up on whiskey. The hood was pulled over Ketchum's head and secured to his coat with horse-blanket pins. "Ready?" Garcia asked.

"Let her go!" Black Jack replied.

It took the wobbly Garcia two swings with his ax to sever the rope and send Ketchum through the drop — a fall so long that his head was jerked loose from his body. Only the tightly pinned hood kept his head from rolling away.

According to one account, a spectator believed that Ketchum had lived through the fall and yelled: "Get another rope for that s.o.b! Let's hang him right this time!"

It seemed a fitting comment on the strange case of the Camp Verde killer, who never received Arizona justice for the murders of Clint Wingfield and R.M. Rodgers. Instead Black Jack was sent to his grave with his head sewn back on, in another territory, for another crime.

# BILL SMITH

The two young men were on foot, leading their horses up a ridge in eastern Arizona. Barely 30 feet away, hidden riflemen fired a barrage of bullets, and the two volunteer lawmen were dead. Bill Smith was blamed for the ambush and the call went out to hunt him down. Also, the savage violence that day,

*March 28, 1900,*

led to the formation of the Arizona Rangers. From then on, Bill Smith was on the run and fighting gunbattle after gunbattle to stay away from the law. Eventually, he disappeared. His mother said he had fled to Argentina.

Bill Smith and his three brothers trekked across the New Mexico border into eastern Arizona in the late 1890s and settled near Springerville in the White Mountains.

The community of St. Johns had its first encounter with him in 1898. Charges of cattle rustling landed him in the local jail, but his stay was short.

Brother Al smuggled a pistol into Bill's cell, and the gang leader was soon free to continue what had made him infamous in New Mexico — holdups, cattle and horse thievery, and killings.

Former Apache County Sheriff Commodore Perry Owens, who had killed three men and wounded another in a gunfight, described the Smith gang as the "toughest bunch to ever drink water from the Hassayampa."

These thugs certainly weren't alone in the realm of lawbreaking in Arizona at that time. But Bill Smith, along with brothers Al, Floyd, and George, seems to have taken particular hold of the public's imagination.

Descriptions of Bill Smith, said to be a handsome, gap-toothed cowpuncher, drip with images of a man who lived the romance of the West.

Even Burt Mossman, the first captain of the Arizona Rangers, described Smith as a person who lived by a strict code of honor.

Writers spoke of Smith in wildly inflated, flowery terms. The *Arizona Daily Star* in 1910 had this to say about the notorious New Mexican:

"An accurate description of the man's deeds and characteristics would make of him, in the eyes of the average romantically inclined maiden, an intensely inter-esting personage, endowed with the most heroic qualities.

"Standing six feet in his socks, with a figure slender but straight as an arrow, firm and regular features, black eyes that flashed with fire and thick black hair, he was almost 35 years of age when he went on the 'scout' back in 1900.

"Whatever his reason for doing so may have been, he succeeded quickly in gathering about him a band of seven other desperate characters, including three brothers, all of whom would have followed him into the jaws of purgatory."

Such grandiose attitudes obscured the cold facts, making it difficult to clearly track the Smith gang's many vile deeds. But reasonable observers, recognizing the incompleteness of the record and the necessity for informed supposition, have attributed to the gang at least five killings, including a member of the newly-formed Arizona Rangers.

The prolonged chase of the Smith gang began March 26, 1900, with the arrival in St. Johns of a mail driver bearing the news that five men had been seen butchering a beef on the road to Springerville. Sheriff Ed Beeler quickly organized a posse and engaged the outlaws at the county bridge three miles west of town.

Although no one in the law party was injured, more than 50 shots were fired and the hunt was on.

By the next morning, Apache County rancher Dick Gibbons was leading a second posse to back up Beeler. Gibbons divided his men into two groups. He headed one of them and told the second group to stay on the rustlers' trail and drive them into his bunch.

The second group — consisting of Dick's nephew, Gus Gibbons, 24, Frank Lesueur, 21, and Antonio Armijo and Frank Ruiz — planned to stay on the rustlers' trail and meet up with Dick Gibbons on the following morning.

The four young men didn't show up for the meeting. Later, Dick Gibbons met Armijo and Ruiz on the trail. The two explained they had quit the hunt the night before, leaving the younger Gibbons and Lesueur alone.

A short time later, Dick Gibbons came to the crest of a gorge covered with boulders and cedar brush. His diary contains a powerful description of what he saw:

"It looked like the body of a man, but I would not admit it to myself. I was still too far away to be able to identify it, and while I was thinking about it I saw another object that looked like a quilt had been thrown away by the outlaws and had been rolled up by the wind and lodged in the wash where it now laid, but as we drew nearer, I saw that it was the body of my nephew Gus Gibbons.

"It was lying in the bottom of a little draw with head

down hill and face upwards, with three ghastly bullet holes through the head. One of them had entered his mouth and had come out the back of his neck. One had gone in at the left ear and had come out below the mouth, breaking the lower jaw and disfiguring the face awfully.

"We well knew what the other object was that we had noticed lying on the hillside. The sight was horrifying to the senses. To see the two boys lying there, boys I had known since they were in the cradle and had watched grow up. They were just in the pink of manhood and for them to be ambushed and shot down like dogs, without even a chance to fight for their lives, made me sick.

"It was murder in its worst form and there is not another crime beneath the roof of heaven that can stain the soul of man with a more infernal hue than an assassination such as this."

The scene was easy to reconstruct. The boys were on foot, leading their horses up the ridge, when the rifles, hidden in ambush barely 30 feet off, opened up. Adding to the horror, the two were robbed of all possessions, including their hats.

Words were inadequate to convey the feelings that gripped St. Johns. As the *St. Johns Herald* wrote:

"Our town is overwhelmed with sadness and two homes are bursting full of grief. Two noble, manly youths have fallen, victims of fiends in human shape."

In Reserve, New Mexico, the next night, the gang stole seven horses and rode off in the direction of the Chiricahua Mountains in southeastern Arizona.

Posses were now in pursuit, but the bad fortune of catching up to them fell to U.S. Marshal George

Scarborough and Deputy Walter Birchfield. A fatal joust occurred April 3 in a remote Chiricahua Mountain spot called Triangle Springs.

According to the *Santa Fe New Mexican* of April 5, 1900, Scarborough and Birchfield were victimized in the same fashion as Gibbons and Lesueur — ambushed by rifle fire. The first volley shattered Marshal Scarborough's leg. Another round struck Birchfield, the deputy, in the arm, but he was still able to build a crude rock wall to protect his wounded comrade.

As soon as darkness cloaked his movements, Birchfield mounted a horse and galloped away in search of assistance. He returned at daybreak to find Scarborough suffering mightily from pain and exposure to overnight rain and snow.

Scarborough, a former Texas Ranger who had once captured famed stage robber Pearl Hart after her escape from a Tucson jail, died at Deming, New Mexico, after surgery to amputate his leg.

For some observers, the identity of the quarry has always been in doubt. Newspapers published the names of numerous suspects, the numbers undoubtedly inflated by the common use of aliases.

Rustlers George Stevenson and James Brooks, recent escapees from jail, were two such suspects. They were captured in Sonora and taken to jail in Silver City, New Mexico. But they escaped on May 28 and were never retaken, leaving the question of their guilt or innocence forever unanswered.

Stevenson and Brooks were said to have been associates of Butch Cassidy's famed Wild Bunch, as was a desperado named Todd Carver. He, too, was named as Scarborough's killer.

As always, however, the Smith gang seemed the most likely perpetrators, and Sheriff Beeler evidently agreed. He traveled to New Mexico to dredge up whatever information he could on the notorious family.

The press pointed a finger at the Smiths, too.

The *Tombstone Prospector* and the *Phoenix Herald* reported that the same men had committed both attacks. *The Prospector* named them, misidentifying Bill Smith as Dick Smith:

"The five men whose names are John Hunter, alias Dick Smith; Bob Johnson; Wilson, alias Smith; Kid Carver and one man unknown ..."

The newspapers wrote of the $2,000 in reward money offered by Apache County, and proudly reported that the outlaws would shortly be intercepted by lawmen.

But capture never came and that didn't sit well with

Dick Gibbons. His outrage at the killings prompted him to run for the Territorial Legislature in the elections of September 1900. Gibbons won the seat by campaigning on the need to form the Arizona Rangers, and the group came into existence in March 1901.

Not surprisingly, its first and deadliest fight was with Bill Smith.

The action started in early October 1901 when the gang was spotted south of Springerville with a herd of stolen horses.

Lawmen organized a posse that included Carlos Tafolla, a Ranger stationed in the area for the sole purpose of keeping watch over the Smiths.

On October 8, after tracking the gang along the Black River in northern Graham County, the posse came to the Smiths' camp, located at the bottom of a draw about 100 feet deep and 200 yards wide.

At dusk the lawmen made their move, crawling to the western peak of the draw. That decision — which put the setting sun at their backs, illuminating them as targets — proved deadly.

Posse member Bill Maxwell, a one-time friend of Bill Smith's, called out: "Bill Smith, we arrest you in the name of the law and the name of the Territory of Arizona, and call upon you and your companions to lay down your arms."

But the gang would have none of that.

In a 1947 interview, former Ranger Joe Pearce, chief of the Apache tribal police at the time of the shoot-out, told what happened next:

"The guns opened up — mostly 30-30s, but Bill

Smith was using a new Savage rifle that shot a .303 bullet. When you got hit with one of them you stayed hit.

"Well, the fight was soon over, but it was plenty hot while it lasted. When the smoke settled the Smiths were high-tailing for the timber.

"Ranger Tafolla was on his back shot twice through the middle and calling for water. Bill Maxwell was dead, the crown of his big hat shot out ..."

Separated from their horses, the Smiths made another escape, dashing away on foot through the mountain snow.

A Ranger posse led by Mossman hurried to the scene and a massive manhunt followed. Among the pursuers was George Scarborough, Jr., son of the recently murdered marshal, who boldly told reporters: "If necessary, I will devote the rest of my life to the capture of the Smith outlaws, one of whom is the slayer of my father."

But with snow obscuring their tracks, the Smiths eluded the Rangers and crossed the border into Mexico. They never again were known to set foot in Arizona.

The only evidence of their later whereabouts came from the boys' mother. She told Pearce that they hopped a boat at Galveston, Texas, and sailed to Argentina.

The Smith saga has two strange postscripts. The first involves the crown of Bill Maxwell's big hat, which remained on the ground for several years, a cloth monument that cowboys were afraid to touch, in a place they called the Battle Ground.

The other concerns the legend of Bill Smith.

Numerous reports state that he grieved at killing Maxwell, and that his gang's intention had been to shoot another posse member with whom they'd been feuding.

According to these stories, Smith insisted that his heartfelt apologies reach Maxwell's mother.

Smith also wrote a letter to Mossman, explaining in great detail what happened in the fight at the deep draw.

These two actions played a large role in furthering Bill Smith's image for chivalry and honor.

But his most enduring legacy was ruthlessness — and the resulting creation of the Arizona Rangers, who operated until 1909, when peace settled over Arizona.

# CHAPTER NINETEEN

# THE GLOBE FIENDS

Everything about the brief criminal careers of
Lafayette Grime and Curtis Hawley went
wrong except their lynching. That was a
model of efficiency. It happened at 2 a.m. on

## August 24, 1882.

The bells of the Methodist Church pealed as
the two men were strung up from Globe's big
sycamore tree. The *Arizona Gazette* boasted
that "not the least disorder occurred and not
a drunken man was seen on the streets."
But even a drunk would have known
that Grime and Hawley were incompetent
outlaws destined for the rope from the day
they plotted their crime.

Lafayette Grime was a slightly built, 19-year-old dance instructor with a reputation for gentleness and feet so small he had to wear women's shoes.

Curtis Hawley, a contractor, was heavy-set with a countenance made brooding by what one writer called beetle brows snaking across his forehead. And he was as cold as a mountain winter. After taking part in a robbery and double murder, Hawley used $80 of the stolen loot to buy a fancy new suit, which he wore to the funeral of the men he helped kill.

The coming together of these unlikely confederates, later dubbed the "Globe fiends," produced five of Gila County's darkest days.

Their bizarre story started on Sunday, August 20, 1882, when Grime and Hawley opened fire on a mule train hauling mail and gold from the Pinal Mountains into Globe. Their plan was to shoot the mule carrying the treasure box, then stage a phony Indian attack by raining bullets over the heads of packer Frank Porter and guard Andy Hall. When the two victims fled, Grime and Hawley would make off with the gold.

The outlaws were aided in their plot by Cicero Grime, a down-on-his-luck photographer and Lafayette's older brother. Under Hawley's orders, the elder Grime was at the summit of the Pinal Mountains when the cargo was loaded onto the mules. Then he rode ahead of the train to tell his partners that the treasure box was indeed heavy, indicating a large cache of gold inside, and that Hall was carrying only a small pistol. But Cicero Grime advised the others to abandon the robbery, something Lafayette was more than willing to do.

Hawley, the plan's mastermind, responded by drawing

his gun and barking, "We came out to get this box and by God, we are going to get it."

Cicero Grime departed and a reluctant Lafayette returned to his ambush perch.

Their plan almost worked. Hawley dropped the treasure-laden mule with a round from his Henry rifle, and the other animals in the train scattered.

Hall yelled back to Porter, "Frank, I'll stay with you, old boy. Don't run."

But after realizing they were under fire from two men, Hall shouted, "There is more than one and we better get out of this!"

Despite their agreement not to shoot the men, Grime panicked and sent a bullet through Hall's thigh and into the mule he was riding. The wounded Wells Fargo guard dismounted and struggled back up the hill, leaving the gold unprotected.

Grime used a hatchet to empty the treasure box of $5,000 to $6,000. Also in the box was a mail shipment. Grime tossed it aside, prompting another dispute with his partner. Hawley wanted him to take the registered mail, arguing that they might be leaving behind as much as $1,000. Grime refused, and the arguing bandits fled on foot along the east slope of the Pinals.

Robbery became murder when the criminals happened upon Dr. Walter Vail, who was riding toward the El Capitan Mine leading a pack horse loaded with supplies.

Vail had heard the shooting and asked about it. When Hawley told him that hostile Indians were raiding and the men were hurrying to escape to Globe, Vail offered the use of his horses. The doctor, described in one account as a "likeable old sawbones," paid dearly for his kindness. A short while later, Hawley fell behind Vail on the trail and shot him as he rode.

Then he turned his gun on Grime and told him to shoot Vail, too. "We are in this thing together and you have got to go as far as I do," Hawley said.

Rotten luck was Vail's undoing, but Hall was done in by bravery.

With a hole in his thigh, this experienced frontiersman, a member of John Wesley Powell's famed 1869 expedition to the Grand Canyon, set out after the robbers.

But Hall was operating on a fatal misconception: he never got a good look at the shooters and assumed they were Indians. When he caught up with Hawley and Grime, Hall dropped his guard and the three men agreed to go together to Globe.

In their written confessions, Grime and Hawley told differing accounts of Hall's subsequent murder, with each man accusing the other of back-shooting and brutality.

Meanwhile, Porter arrived in Globe with news of the attack, and within minutes a posse was riding into the mountains.

Vail was discovered, still alive, with Hall's rolled-up coat under his head. The dying doctor was able only to tell deputies that he'd been shot by two men, one tall and dark complexioned.

Andy Hall was found nearby in the tall grass. His body was riddled with eight bullet holes. The *Arizona Silver Belt* reported that "Hall's breast was exposed, his clothing saturated with blood and so many wounds in sight that a hasty glance was all that was necessary to show that more than one man had done the work."

The dead men were brought to town and laid out at

the Wells Fargo office on Pine Street. Virtually every citizen of Globe came to witness the shocking sight. Revenge was coming.

Monday and Tuesday were days of mourning, rumor, and investigation. But it took very little of the latter for U.S. Deputy Marshal Pete Gabriel to settle on Lafayette Grime as a suspect.

Incredibly, Grime had borrowed a new pistol from Globe lawman Dan Lacey the day before the crime, and he returned it uncleaned.

The normally sociable Grime was absent from the general excitement in town those two days.

Gabriel located the suspect at a mine outside town Tuesday evening. Grime quickly confessed, then named his two accomplices, including his brother. Hawley was arrested at his cabin and he confessed, too.

A bitter jurisdictional dispute followed the arrests. Marshal Gabriel wanted to spirit the men out of Gila County on charges of robbing the U.S. mail, and spare them a lynching in Globe. But Sheriff W.W. Lowther refused to allow the men to leave Gila County without answering murder charges.

The lawmen agreed to let District Attorney J.D. McCabe decide who had jurisdiction. He sided with Lowther.

Before turning over his prisoners, Gabriel shook hands with them and said, "I am sorry, boys, you will be lynched within an hour after you reach Globe."

Charles Clark, a posse member who wrote about the events 30 years later in the *Arizona Republican*, described the scene in Globe at 7 p.m. on Wednesday when Gila

County lawmen returned to Globe with the prisoners:

"As we passed each successive saloon, we were recognized and men poured out in crowds — each man with a 'long Tom' or 'Henry' rifle in his hand. The crowd reached the jail about as quickly as we did, and for a few moments it looked as though Gabriel had over-estimated their time in his prediction. ... We shoved them in (to the jail), just as four men came up, bearing a cottonwood log for a battering ram.

"By this time the crowd numbered 200 or more, with recruits coming every moment. ... Sheriff Lowther was swept to one side, the end of the log hit the door of the jail and knocked it off its fastenings. A dozen men jumped in and grabbed Hawley and Grime, ropes were produced and the cry, 'Hang the damn murderers!' came from a hundred frenzied throats."

In their book, *Globe, Arizona,* authors Clara T. Woody and Milton L. Schwartz wrote that Lowther agreed to bring his prisoners before Justice of the Peace George Allen, if the mob allowed a hearing to take place.

The raucous and emotional session was held in a nearby hall with spectators practically hanging out the windows. The evidence presented was indisputable, and Allen ruled that the prisoners should be held for trial in Superior Court.

But the mob, reminded of Hawley's bold appearance at the funerals of Hall and Vail, was even more righteous in its cause and took control of the killers again.

The *Arizona Gazette* of August 31, 1882, described what happened next:

"The prisoners asked for three hours' time and promised to reveal the hidden place of the stolen money. This was acceded to and then, in company with about 30 citizens, they repaired to the foothills of the Pinal Mountains about four miles from town and there pointed out the hiding place of the money."

The mob's absence allowed Lowther to hustle Cicero Grime away to a cave off McCormick Wash. The rescue undoubtedly saved Grime's life because the mob had discovered the money divided into three parts, apparently implicating Cicero.

Cicero later was sentenced to a 21-year term at Yuma Prison. After a brief time there, he was sent to an insane asylum in California, but he escaped after a month and was never recaptured.

The mob returned to Globe just after midnight, and so did their cries to "Hang the murderers!"

After Hawley made out his will in Allen's courtroom, Clark wrote, "The crowd formed into a hollow square with the prisoners in the center, each with a rope around his neck, marching down Broad Street" to the sycamore tree outside St. Elmo's Saloon.

The condemned men spent their final moments demonstrating once again just how mismatched they were.

When the Rev. D.W. Calfee asked if he should pray for them, Grime said yes.

But Hawley, surly to the last, responded: "What the hell do I care for the hereafter? It's this damned mob I want to be rid of."

Then, as the hands of a dozen angry citizens prepared to yank back the ropes, Grime's body went limp and the youngster collapsed against the noose.

"It was conclusively proven," Clark wrote, "that

this 19-year-old boy died of fright before the rope was tightened."

Hawley wasn't about to go easily. His noose was askew, and Clark wrote that it caused him to writhe "under the limb for ten or fifteen minutes, slowly strangling to death, fairly whistling at each breath as does a horse when choked at the snubbing post."

An angry Lowther, saying he had nothing to do with the lynching, simply left the dead men there. They dangled from that big sycamore until 2 p.m. Thursday, making Day Five of the incident the blackest of all.

# PEARL HART

Two figures on horses lurk at a bend in the road in
Cane Springs Canyon, north of Florence, Arizona.
They wait to hold up the stage bound for Globe.
One is Joe Boot. Eventually he's captured and
sentenced to 30 years in prison.
The other — slightly built, with long hair
tucked into a white sombrero — wears
a gray shirt and dungarees, and packs
a .38-caliber revolver. This is Pearl Hart, a
luckless and downtrodden creature who's
been driven to this deed by desperation.
The robbery that day,

*May 30, 1899,*

thrusts her to immortality. Her act would be
seen as a blow for women's rights.
Indeed, Pearl Hart stirred the imaginations
of men and women across the country.
Even the jury that tried her succumbed
to her charms and acquitted her.

Pearl Taylor was 16 when she eloped from an Ontario boarding school with a charming two-bit gambler named Hart. But she found little glamour in drifting around cheap hotels, bars, and race tracks, and left him. Shortly after, he talked her into going with him to the 1893 World's Columbian Exposition in Chicago. There, she became entranced with the Wild West Show, and when the fair was over, she left Hart again and headed for Trinidad, Colorado, and a new life.

Finding no romance as a cook and domestic, Pearl drifted into Arizona, bearing a baby boy. Two years after she left him, the inept gambler appeared in Phoenix and promised to find a job. Pearl went back with him. They were happy for about three years, and a little girl was born to them. But when Hart started abusing her, Pearl sent her children to her mother and took a job as a servant in the East.

Two years later, she again succumbed to Hart's entreaties and went with him to live in Tucson, where he loafed, squandered Pearl's savings, and abused her. Pearl left him again, and in 1898 he joined McCord's Regiment of Rough Riders.

Pearl returned to a miserable life in Phoenix, and she tried to commit suicide several times. Finally she found a job as cook at a mining camp at Mammoth, where she lived in a tent on the edge of a river. After a few months her health forced her to give it up. Packing her belongings into a wagon, she set out for Globe. But even the elements were against her, and the horses were unable to pull the wagon through the mud. Defeated, she returned to Mammoth. There, she had a small bit of luck. She met Joe Boot, who also wanted to go to Globe, and he helped her get there.

Pearl found a job at a miners' boarding house, but one of the big mines shut down, and her job ended. Nevertheless, when one of her brothers wrote that he was in trouble and needed money desperately, kind-hearted Pearl couldn't refuse, and sent all she had.

Then her husband was mustered out of the Army and showed up again at her doorstep. This time, however, she bought him a bottle of whisky and sent him on his way.

When it seemed that nothing else could go wrong,

another letter arrived, stating that Pearl's mother was dying. "That letter drove me crazy," Pearl said. "No matter what I had been, my mother had been my dearest, truest friend, and I longed to see her again before she died." But she had no money for the trip, and she had no prospects.

Then Joe Boot, who would do anything for Pearl, obtained a mining claim. The two of them struggled with pick and shovel, exhausted themselves, but didn't find a bit of color in the claim.

Pearl was frantic. It was then that Joe suggested they rob the Globe stage. It would be easy, he said, and no one would be hurt. Pearl was shocked at first, but desperation weakened her resolve. "Joe," she said finally, "if you will promise me that no one will be hurt, I'll go with you."

And so on that spring day in 1899, Pearl Hart and Joe Boot waited for the Globe stage to round the bend at Cane Springs Canyon. They heard the vehicle rattling in the ruts, the trace chains jingling, and then it was there. As the pair cocked and aimed their pistols, the driver reined in the team with a jolt. The dozing passengers flew out of their seats and landed in a heap.

"Throw up your hands!" shouted Joe.

"Raise 'em," Pearl's small voice echoed.

Joe told Pearl to dismount and search the three passengers for guns. They had been so frightened that they had left their guns inside the coach. Pearl found them, gave a Colt .45 to Joe, and kept a .44 for herself.

"Search 'em," said Joe.

A short, fat man was shaking so much that Pearl had trouble getting into his pockets, but they finally yielded $390. A "dude," with his hair parted in the middle, gave up

$36, and a Chinese man, who was nearer Pearl's size and "scared to death," parted with $5. The robbers gave each of them one dollar, and ordered them to move on and not look back.

Instead of heading for the railroad and the border, the novice bandits turned their horses into the most inaccessible terrain they could find, attempting to throw off pursuers. But Joe and Pearl lost their way several times, and at nightfall, when they emerged on a highway, they discovered they were only a mile from where they had committed the robbery.

Other misfortunes followed.

With a posse on their trail, they crept into a small cave, only to be confronted by the shining eyes of a wild boar. Then Joe nearly drowned when his worn-out mount failed to jump a ditch. Torrential rains followed. Soaked, exhausted, and miserable, they fell asleep beneath a canopy of trees. A few hours later they were aroused by rifles prodding their ribs.

Pearl was furious at first, but when she saw the fascination in the eyes of the posse, she began to undergo a change. She told her story with a flair as she shared the sheriff's horse to Benson, and during the train ride to Casa Grande and Florence she held audiences spellbound.

After years of struggle and rejection, people were admiring her. "Would you do it again?" asked one charmed onlooker. "Damn right, Podner," she replied, swaggering.

The public loved it. During her stay in the Florence jail she became a celebrity, a symbol of "contemporary wild western womanhood," driven to desperation by love and a dying mother. She saw that boldness paid off and sent a note to the prosecuting attorney: "I shall not consent to be tried under a law which my sex had no voice in making." The suffragette movement took up her cry, stimulating debate throughout the nation.

All this was too much for the sheriff. He shipped Pearl off to Tucson, where she was locked in a room in the Pima County Courthouse. There, a fellow prisoner proposed that they escape and form an outlaw band. She declined, but he broke her out anyway, and they fled to New Mexico. They were captured in October near Deming, New Mexico, where, according to a newspaper account, Pearl was "starting a gang of which she was to be the bandit queen."

Shipped back to the Pima County Jail, she awaited arraignment in Florence, where Joe Boot still languished.

Love bloomed again in June for Pearl and Joe when they were united in Florence. The *Yuma Sun* reported that "Boot stretches his hand through the bars for the girl to caress and they seem happy."

Joe and Pearl were tried separately. Joe was sentenced to 30 years for highway robbery. Pearl's jurors, however, apparently were charmed by her. Although she was positively identified by the stage's passengers and driver, and she never took the stand to deny her guilt, the jury returned in 10 minutes with a verdict of acquittal. In frustration, the judge directed the prosecutor to re-arraign Pearl on a charge of stealing a revolver from the driver. She was found guilty of that charge and sentenced to five years in the territorial prison in Yuma.

In a facility built for male prisoners, Pearl proved to be a headache for her jailers, especially when she espoused religion, lectured on the evils of crime, and once more stirred up public support. In a year and a half she was pardoned by Governor A.O. Brodie.

She left for Kansas City, where her enterprising sister proposed to cast her in a play entitled *Arizona Bandit*. Now Pearl could perform on a real stage.

But the play fizzled, and Pearl never appeared before the footlights. In fact, she dropped out of sight. There was one report that she had been arrested on a minor offense in Kansas City in 1904. Later, she wrote a poem about her stage robbery and gave it to reporters. But then Pearl Hart seemed to vanish.

Twenty years later, it is told, a gray-haired woman showed up at the Pima County Courthouse and asked an attendant if she could "look the place over." When asked why, the woman replied that she had lived there years ago.

As she was shown around, the woman nodded and smiled. "Well," she said, "it hasn't changed much."

The attendant, now curious, asked the woman's name.

"Pearl Hart," the visitor replied, and then she was gone again.

# Arizona As Only Arizon

## Let's go!

### With guidebooks filled with information and color photos

**Tucson To Tombstone**
In this guidebook, avid southeastern Arizona explorer Tom Dollar tells stories of the region and takes you over its trails. As you learn facts and legends of the Old West, you'll travel from desert floor to riparian canyons to alpine forests atop majestic mountains. Features maps, travel tips, and more than 128 full-color photographs. Softcover. 96 pages.
**#ATTS6 $12.95**

**Arizona Ghost Towns and Mining Camps**
Ghost town authority Philip Varney brings the Old West to life with captivating anecdotes and a gallery of rare, historic photographs. Regional maps, detailed travel information, and a full-color photographic portfolio tell what each site is like today and make this fascinating history of Arizona's mining boom a reliable travel guide as well. 136 pages. Softcover. **#AZGS4 $14.95**

**We Call It "Preskit"**
Explore the frontier history and home-town charm of Prescott and the high country of central Arizona with author Jack August. The full-color book features the things to see and do in the area, including Jerome. Softcover. 64 Pages.
**#APRS6 $12.95**

**Arizona's 144 Best Campgrounds**
Written and photographed by Arizona outdoorsman James Tallon, this guidebook groups campgrounds into eight regions. For each region there are maps locating campsites and charts summarizing facilities and fishing opportunities at or near each site. 160 full-color photographs. Softcover. 192 pages. **#ACPS6 $13.95**

## Ordering Information
**To order these and other books and products write to:**
*Arizona Highways*, 2039 West Lewis Avenue, Phoenix, AZ 85009-2893.
Or send a fax to 602-254-4505. Or call toll-free nationwide 1-800-543-5432.
(In the Phoenix area or outside the U.S., call 602-258-1000.)
Visit us at http://www.arizhwys.com/ to order online.

# *Highways* Can Present It
## Let's read!
### About the good, the bad, and the rotten

**Manhunts & Massacres**
Pieced together from the annals of Arizona's frontier days, here are 18 stories recounting cleverly staged ambushes, massacres that cried out for justice, and the valiant, sometimes vicious, pursuits staged by lawmen and Indian fighters. Softcover. 144 pages. **#AMMP7 $7.95**

**Days Of Destiny**
This book features 20 historical stories about Arizona's worst desperados, the lawmen who brought them to justice, and how Fate changed their lives. Gathered by *Arizona Highways* from more than 70 years of writing about the Old West. Softcover. 144 pages. **#ADAP6 $7.95**

**Law Of The Gun**
Historian and author Marshall Trimble presents an overview of those who wielded the gun to break the law, those who embraced the gun to uphold it, and the guns they used. You'll marvel at the stories of such compelling figures as Wyatt Earp, Wild Bill Hickok, Kit Carson, John Wesley Hardin, Jesse James, the Daltons, and Judge Roy Bean. Includes 20 historic photos. Softcover. 192 pages. **#AGNP7 $8.95**

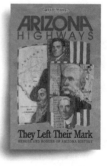

**They Left Their Mark: Heroes and Rogues of Arizona History**
These larger-than-life characters have boldly written their names on the pages of Arizona history. From the early Spanish explorer Juan Bautista de Anza to land swindler James Addison Reavis to World War II Marine hero Ira Hayes, *They Left Their Mark* presents fascinating biographies of Arizona's famous and infamous. Softcover. 144 pages. **#ATMP7 $7.95**

**SPECIAL OFFER FOR ALL FOUR WILD WEST SERIES BOOKS!**
Order all four Wild West books shown above for only **$24.95.**
You save $7.85! **#ADPST7** Order for yourself... or for someone who loves the Old West. *Note: Quantities are limited. Order Today!*